Origin Stories

Also by Corinna Vallianatos

The Beforeland: A Novel
My Escapee: Stories

Origin Stories

Stories

CORINNA VALLIANATOS

Graywolf Press

Published by Graywolf Press
212 Third Avenue North, Suite 485
Minneapolis, Minnesota 55401

www.graywolfpress.org

Published in the United States of America

ISBN 978-1-64445-321-6   (paperback)
ISBN 978-1-64445-322-3   (ebook)

2 4 6 8 9 7 5 3 1
First Graywolf Printing, 2025

Library of Congress Cataloging-in-Publication Data

Names: Vallianatos, Corinna, author.
Title: Origin stories : stories / Corinna Vallianatos.
Description: Minneapolis, Minnesota : Graywolf Press, 2025.
Identifiers: LCCN 2024033423 (print) | LCCN 2024033424 (ebook) |
    ISBN 9781644453216 (paperback) | ISBN 9781644453223 (ebook)
Subjects: LCGFT: Short stories.
Classification: LCC PS3622.A48 O75 2025 (print) | LCC PS3622.A48
    (ebook) | DDC 813/.6—dc23/eng/20240816
LC record available at https://lccn.loc.gov/2024033423
LC ebook record available at https://lccn.loc.gov/2024033424

Cover design: Alban Fischer

Cover art: Juan Moyano / Getty Images

To my parents

Contents

Origin Stories

New Girls

We stole away to be alone. To the bathroom off the rare book reading room, beside the garbage chute on the breezeway of our old dorm, deep in the dining hall's soup-smelling corridor. If someone came in while we were hunched in our stall—it did happen occasionally—we twisted around so our shoes were pointing in the right direction and waited. What they did was banal. They washed their hands and left.

Of course we knew we could be that person. We knew we could be free.

It came at too great a cost to consider this. We'd consider it later. It was 10:00 a.m. and the light was bright in the stall and the bowl had the milky gleam of baby teeth. It was 1:14 p.m. and the light was like a sheet spread over a bed, buoyant with daytime. It was 9:50 p.m. and we rinsed our mouths and spat into the sink, flipped the switch and stepped into the darkness and in the second it took our eyes to adjust to the arm of pale yellow coming from down the corridor, that second of hesitation in which to step forward would be to step into a projector's fiery eye, we perceived quick flicking images of limbs,

3

a scrawl of hair, the branches of trees clothed and then naked, the sun jerking across the sky. We perceived the passage of time.

It wasn't grand or unknowable. Time would pass us forward too. Could this be what we were hiding from?

A question for group and our stalwart leader, though Emily did not often take a philosophical tack in our discussions. Emily was the sensible young doctoral student charged with guiding us in group therapy. She wore round wire-rimmed glasses and black cloth Chinese slippers and sat in an armchair with her legs crossed twice, the toe of the crossed leg tucked again behind the other leg's ankle. Her voice was low and steady and her expression so unflappable we knew she viewed us as specimens, neither wretched nor righteous, and found ourselves wishing for a stronger reaction from her, a little human shock. But it was also that unflappability that gave us ease in the room where we met.

The room was located in the counseling center on Brandon Street at the edge of campus. The Spanish department and language houses were on that street. Once from a window one of our TA's arms waved so frantically and his voice called such an eager *hallooo* it occurred to us that other people were lonely too. Then the automatic doors heaved open and we clapped down the cold corridor to the room where we met with its corduroy couch and bowlegged coffee table and bouquet of silk flowers of no type we could identify though we could see that they were pretty things, meant to please, with pipe cleaner stamens dotted at the tips with clear glass beads.

We liked to sit on the rug and braid and stroke its fringe. It was possible we made ourselves suffer just to be there. We felt we deserved to suffer and so we sought out others who suffered. We could not see our own suffering but we could see a mark drawn across what was human in each other.

Who were we? We were an ex-model who had escaped her abusive father in a rowboat across the choppy waters of the Chesapeake Bay. We were a premed student who had discovered that a cat she was dissecting was pregnant, miniature cats tucked in a row inside the mother, and that what she would have to do from here on out was look upon a whole and think of it as parts, that she would have to savage it. We were an art history major in possession of an excellent cable-knit cardigan who had gone on a shopping spree at a downtown boutique and bought hundreds and hundreds of dollars' worth of clothing, indecorous bags of it. Dressing rooms, she said, were like confessionals. You saw a private vision of yourself. The privacy of the vision *was* the absolution. Still, she had returned everything except the cardigan. We were a wannabe writer who had been house-sitting for a neighbor and had stood in the neighbor's kitchen and eaten an entire box of the neighbor's Godiva chocolates without enjoying them at all, even the seashell filled with hazelnut cream which was the very chocolate she used to select with her mother at the Godiva counter at the mall, an act so ritualized it was basically religious, the comfort of being with her mother, the crinkle of the bag in which the chosen chocolate was nestled, its striated body— imagine figuring out how to mold in chocolate a perfect replica of a seashell, imagine bending to a task meant only to create pleasure— how slowly she had bitten into it and let the hazelnut melt on her tongue, and now, ten years later, after shoving all of the neighbor's chocolates into her mouth she placed the empty box back into the cabinet as if nothing had happened. She thought she was invisible, the wannabe writer continued. And she did whatever she could to stay that way, binged, purged, took laxatives. Three or four blue pills and then sometime in the middle of the night, a liquid waterfall of shit.

And there was me. I didn't know how to talk about myself. I suspect it's that I was ashamed of my existence.

We walked together through the wind. Walked through neighborhoods where professors and their families lived. How different we would be, we thought, had we grown up here with parents who were generous and eccentric rather than worried and downtrodden and cruel. Our longing took in each broad porch, each dignified old car, each *Times* slanted across the sidewalk like the hand of a clock.

We attended the screening of a documentary about a woman who was in love with an amusement park ride. She had loved an archery bow before that in a sexual manner we were meant to believe. At the reception afterward we sucked at the fleshy pulp of strawberries. I get the Scrambler, a woman standing near us said. It's got a lot of sort of outstretched *appendages*. Girth, velocity, her friend said. Heft, speed. And there was Emily, her back to us. Should we approach her? Why shouldn't we acknowledge her with a nod, a brief pleasantry? We felt very mature as we filed over to say hello, threading our way through people laughing with stuff in their teeth, drinking wine and letting crumbs darken their shirts. We passed great mounds of cheese. Tables piled with crackers and brownies. Just then Emily turned to the man she was with (all the worse that he was our type, tall and rumpled, his glasses askew) and jabbed her thumb over her shoulder in our direction and said in a wry, conspiratorial voice, My bulimic girls.

We froze. It was like a slap for daring to walk among people who did not do the disgusting things we did to ourselves. Then turned all at once in the opposite direction, wishing for the trapdoor, the quick exit.

I dropped the cheese cube I was holding into my coat pocket. The handful of cubes.

The next morning we met to debate the issue of Emily. The premed student said we must calmly confront her about what we'd heard. The ex-model thought not and she lived on the lawn, in the room next to Edgar Allan Poe's, so clearly she was smart. (How did she stand the tourists gawking through the glass door at Poe's old rickety bed, pressing the button to hear the informative Poe script read with fixed jollity over and over again?) We should forgive her for her mistake, the ex-model said, as she forgives us.

She doesn't forgive us, the wannabe writer said. She just bears witness. She too cast her vote for confronting Emily, though not with the restraint the premed student proposed. Wasn't there frankly something a little badass about what we did? You had to have nerve at the very least. If we confronted Emily we would be announcing the vitality in ourselves, telling her to make way for us motherfuckers.

Maybe this was why she wanted to be a writer, so she might turn every humiliating moment into something larger, stronger, more lasting. And the regular moments too, the diner table we sat around and the clatter of silverware and the scrape of spatulas on flat-top grills and the room seeming to fish-eye a little with the weight and heat of hungry bodies. We saluted her, we did, but it also made us uneasy, for those moments, memorialized, would be harder to discard, and often we wanted to throw everything away.

The art history major asked if anyone'd considered that Emily might suspect we'd overheard her. And if so, shouldn't she be the one to address what'd happened? Shouldn't she apologize? We would debase ourselves further if we didn't wait for her to address it. Of course, that's what we did well, wasn't it? Debase ourselves? We laughed at this, at the truth of it. The waitress came to our table and we ordered more coffee. At a neighboring table, a group of boys our age, their hair still tousled from sleep, aimed ketchup bottles over mounds of hash browns and slapped the bottoms with the heels of their hands. The sound was so impotent we wanted to spring to our feet and show them how to pry the first slide of ketchup out with a butter knife. They were not unintelligent but we might so gracefully and thoroughly oversee them.

In group the next day the conversation sputtered and ground to a halt. Those who had been in favor of confronting Emily said nothing. Those who had not been in favor wished those who had been would just go ahead and do it.

You're quiet today, Emily said.

We were far away, in our stalls. The bathroom door opening.

The girls who entered and went on their way. We went with them.

To Christmas parties at fraternities hung with wreaths. Snow falling outside, soft and sparkling, and inside, in the large, high-ceilinged rooms, the mantelpiece busts wore Santa hats. A partygoer danced by in velvet pants that caused us to blush with admiration. We wore a gray wool skirt with low-top Converse and a red halter dress we had had hemmed for the occasion and a black lace shirt tucked into jeans. We were so aware of the strangeness of our surroundings we had an apprehension of another force, practically, like a congregant moved to stand and praise god, and indeed what we felt was a kind of belief.

We weren't on the list but someone had let us in. We were on the list and someone had let us in. We weren't on the list but we weren't not on the list either.

At semester's end the art history major announced that she would not be returning for the next. She was entering a treatment program. We bid her goodbye with a big bag of candy, jellybeans jangling against syrup-filled raspberries. This was not perversity but an act of love. We had never received love in the form of food, or not for a very long time. We didn't want to blame our mothers for everything, but if only our mothers had urged us to eat instead of not! If only our mothers had stocked the refrigerator with treats for us as they did for our brothers, vanilla ice cream and root beer and lasagna! Then we might be able to stop using rueful exclamation marks!

We went home to a big white-brick Colonial with black shutters and a vinyl-sided split-level with scudding clouds of dog slobber on the front window and a town house on a gaslit cobblestone street. The wannabe writer stopped writing. The premed student slept. The ex-model rose in the cold black and took the train to New York to model again. At our first group back, she bent to her knapsack and pulled out a crumpled letter stamped with an upside-down flag. It was a letter from her father, and she wondered if she might read it to us.

Emily said we'd run out of time and we'd have to shelve it for next week. Shelve it! The dispassion.

The next week, the ex-model produced the letter again. *Dear Dolly*, she read. She looked up.

Dolly's something he calls me, she said.

Dear Dolly, I loved you before you were born. When you were a little girl you hated to run. You would pretend to run but you would not actually run for any reason. My main piece of advice for you is don't give out your phone number and don't be a tease. They claim not to but I believe the ones that are know it and are happy about it. Very pleased. I'm going to buy you a jeep. Love, Dad.

She made a production of ripping the letter up and letting the pieces flurry into her lap. Emily said she had done the right thing by not replying and the ex-model laughed. But she had, she said, she had replied. God, she was so pathetic. She had called him and left a message with the secretary he'd been having an affair with for as long as she could remember, a woman who used to be sent on errands to buy her school supplies, her highlighters and tights, and who blatantly considered her unworthy.

I said if only she had run a little . . .

Emily turned to me sharply and said this wasn't a joke, it was someone's life.

The ex-model said it was fine, it was good to be able to laugh about it.

But Emily was right. I had seen an in and I had taken it. When I saw ins I thought I must take them.

We stayed in town that summer. We drove to the reservoir to swim and went to the hospital to have our electrolyte levels checked. School started again. We were third years, fourth years. The art history major returned to group only to announce that she didn't need group anymore. One of her dietitians had really been awesome. Her name was Zephyr and she had a jawline like a scythe and she taught her that Georgia O'Keeffe's flowers weren't vaginas but poured pancake batter. The premed student stopped coming next. Emily told us she had emailed and shared that group conflicted with lab and that she would miss us and wished us the very best. We doubted that. Perhaps that was what she had said but her meaning would have been different, sharper, more rueful. She knew us and we knew her, and that bond would not so easily, so politely come undone. More likely she had tired of hearing about our sickness, wanted to tend to hers with the little lantern of her obsession. The wannabe writer was writing again, a novella in verse. It was obviously tough going. The ex-model was upset that New York dressed her in Lanz nightgowns and puffer jackets. New York saw her as the kind of girl who withstood gales and went to bed earl—

Bring the pictures, we begged, and it was as we suspected, she was dressed in other things too, pretty things. Dresses that'd get ripped to smithereens in bad weather.

See? we said, but she just smiled shyly and went home for the weekend and while she was there her father shot and killed her and her mother and himself.

We had depended on her beauty. Depended on it to convince ourselves that we weren't completely monstrous, for if we were, surely a person like her wouldn't spend time with us. She had traveled, she knew things. She had taught us how to eat sushi, how to mix the soy sauce and wasabi. Emily cried as we spoke. So here was the shock. We didn't want it anymore. We told her about hearing her call us her bulimic girls. The ex-model took it the hardest, we said. But she didn't blame you, we blamed you. She wanted to protect you. Emily leaned over and tugged a tissue from the box on the coffee table. She blew her nose and a calmness came over her.

Only very simple people are appeased so thoroughly by a nose-blowing, I thought.

We all have our own memories of her, Emily said.

She brought in new girls. They were not reticent as we supposed they should be. They had froggy trumpeting voices and smelled like scented tampons. One of them was a married grad student with a perm. She announced that her husband had asked her to stop for him and so she was never going to do it again. Emily said that was a lot of pressure he was putting on her. She said he should want her to stop for her sake.

But when you are married, the grad student said, you *are* the other. You are basically one body.

I hurt myself, I hurt him. Do you understand? It's not just me I'm dealing with. I'm walking around with a blade to my heart.

Traveling Light

The ex I missed didn't miss me, and the ex who missed me I didn't miss in return. This was probably the way of life but it was frustrating. The ex I missed returned my emails politely but not promptly, his tone faintly self-pitying. He was overworked, he wrote, and busy, much too busy to keep up with old friends. The ex who missed me expressed his nostalgia openly, unselfconsciously, in a stream of texts like his long-ago postcards from Spain that described a small fish on his plate with as much care as the sea as a bullfighting ring as the gorge one looked down upon in Ronda. Words were nothing; they simply slipped out. I had broken up with the ex I missed because I took solace in this. (I was scared of my life then.) When I did so, the ex I missed informed me that I'd regret the decision. I already do, I said, a line designed to elicit hesitation for had he hesitated I'd have leapt back to him—a bad habit, I realized, to need the specter of the wound to sew me closed again—but he turned and left, and I was aware as I watched from my bedroom window his figure in a blue windbreaker grow smaller and smaller that something had changed beyond the way we encountered one another, that some shellacked sun had dipped below the horizon. We slept together once more, while I was still with the ex who missed me. I went to the ex I missed's apartment explicitly to do so. It was very cold, and he played a song I liked that rose and warbled beyond the blankets and whose articulate melancholy heightened my dissatisfaction. I was always dissatisfied then, and I didn't know, I hadn't yet realized that it was the nature of young womanhood itself that was dissatisfying, that I longed to feel a gathering authority but found instead that I grew more uncertain, more doubtful every day. The sex was strangely banal (I'd hoped it would be operatically cathartic). Afterward, in a frigid bathroom filled with the toiletries of men, rust-ringed shaving cream cans and toothbrushes with splayed bristles, as I searched my face for relief or guilt, I realized I'd been so intent on enabling the act that I'd taken away no impression of it. But I remained dogged by him even after we graduated from college, after the ten-year mark had passed, and now the twenty. He did nothing to encourage me. Finally I arranged to visit a friend who lived in the town where he lived, the town where we'd gone to college and where what I've described took place.

I flew to Charlottesville in October. It was too dark to see the foliage from the plane but I assumed it winked below us as we landed. My friend's house was large and empty, with multiple white-brick soot-singed fireplaces whose mantels bore untouched sets of candlesticks. Jolie was a surgeon and her husband worked in finance in London. They had an open marriage, which meant, she explained as she led me to one of the guest rooms, that he dated young Polish and Ukrainian women while she operated on hernias. We sprawled across a blow-up mattress. "It's not as bad as it sounds," she said. "It means I don't have to pick up his dirty socks where he tosses them right *next* to the laundry hamper."

"That's the saddest thing I've ever heard," I said.

"Honestly, I'm grateful to them."

Jolie was beautiful, her black hair shot through with sparks of white, her eyes large and liquid. I was not. I supposed sometimes I looked fine, but usually I appeared startled or confused. I spent most of my time in sweatpants, writing press releases and marketing material for the Thermos company from my home near Los Angeles. Often I did not see anyone between trips to the grocery store. I had never been married. I had no pets. It was either a brazenly simple or an incalculably taxing life, depending on my mood. I had gotten away with something or been deprived of something. My solitude a buoy or a weight, my little house a sanctuary or a cell.

Jolie said her husband liked to keep her informed of the sexual habits of the young women he dated, their startling displays of virtuosity in some acts and prudish disdain for others, like passing gas or the sound of bodies slapping together. "They say it activates their gag reflex," she said. "They have hyperactive gag reflexes."

I had met Jolie's husband only at their wedding, and I remembered how, when he hugged me, he turned his head in the opposite direction, as if scanning the horizon for someone or something that might come and save him.

"Why does he tell you this stuff?" I asked.

"He says they like his gut. He says they scramble over him like Lilliputians," she said, and I was struck by the ego and absurdity of lust, though I had once acted in such ways myself. We talked a little more and she left the room. I changed into a long-sleeved T-shirt and moved my bare legs back and forth between the sheets. The loneliness this town had made me feel twenty years ago curled through me again. It presented a vision of something I knew, something I recognized but would never have, a kind of perfection that I'd seen in the windows of the stately houses on the other end of the city where I grew up, the bright wall of beauty and well-being. Something swift and lovely glimpsed on the other side: a shoulder in a fuzzy sweater, the licorice-black sheen of a piano's raised lid. On the end of Alexandria where I grew up there were brown apartment buildings and a creek that flooded its banks every now and then and went lapping over the grass next to it, all the way up to the jogging path where exercise equipment stood at intervals like the equipment in a prison yard. There was the drainage pipe where my friends and I had played, where a man had come once and roared and flapped his arms and chased us away. I could still see his figure, outlined at the mouth of the pipe against the yellow day. A moth raising its brawny wings.

The next morning, I rose unrested and went to a coffee shop I'd frequented with the ex I missed. The place was full, as it always had been, of glossy, casually disheveled heads, but whereas the heads used to be buried in novels or the city paper now they bent religiously over the screens of laptops and phones. They would sacrifice everything to this glow, their chance to be a serious person, for when you got a glimpse of what it was they were looking at it was usually something like a cat slapping a baby's head. I ordered a coffee. And then he came in and I felt a shock of completion fall through me and a little disappointment I couldn't explain, and he yanked his white earbuds out and doubled the cord over the back of his neck and I saw it wasn't him, it was a younger man wearing an expression of mild hostility. The ex I missed could be peevish, too. How unhappy he'd been when I won a scholarship from the English department instead of him! He considered himself a better writer than me, I'd realized not with indignation but with guilt, for it did not take much to convince me of my unworthiness. I left the coffee shop and walked a few blocks to a restaurant owned by the ex I missed's old roommate. The old roommate feigned not to remember me. He said he was an expert muffuletta maker and I should come back when he was open. I felt a last-ditch flirtation in his gaze.

I walked to the department where the ex I missed taught, having stayed in town long enough to finagle a job at the university we'd attended. The lawn had been the site of a march of white supremacists, an ugly spectacle of men in chinos chanting and carrying torches, and I wondered why permission had been granted for the march in the first place. It had given the men a groomed backdrop on which to stage their hate, albeit a backdrop that didn't admit Black students until 1955 and women until 1970, so not, admittedly, a bastion of progressivism. Were these new waters running from an old fountain or something else entirely? A strain of vileness unique to this age? Surely the university could've denied the march for public safety reasons. I had followed it from California in a deep depression, and had been tempted to text him about it, but had not. Now I skirted the portico's fat columns, went inside, and climbed a flight of stairs to the second floor of the building's old wing, which was attached by a glassed-in walkway to a new, modern wing. I wandered past faculty offices praying to avoid professors who'd been there when I was a student all the while glancing surreptitiously at nameplates, crossed the walkway, which afforded a nice view of the serpentine walls of the gardens, and located the ex I missed's office at the far end of the new wing across from a bathroom. (It was possible that its position denoted a lowly stature.) I knocked on the door, though I could tell by the quality of silence that crept from beneath it—a mist of disuse—that he wasn't there. If I'd thought he *was* there, I'd have waited for him to emerge, I'd've never knocked to announce myself after so many years. There were no cartoons or postcards or flyers taped to it, and its bareness in contrast to the busy papered-over utility-pole aspect of the other doors was such a pure demonstration of his personality I was nearly felled by it. A student wearing pearly glasses came to a stop next to me.

"Do you work here?" she said.

She said *work* like anyone could do anything.

"I used to."

"So you know your way around?"

"Not really."

That night, Jolie ordered pizza. She poured us full glasses of wine.

"Apparently Patrick's women wear shaping girdles," she said. "They wear compression underwear."

I pinched up a clot of cheese and mushroom and olive, and popped it into my mouth. "What a waste."

"But don't you remember being young? All the warping pressures?"

"Of course I do," I said.

"I could put my foot down. I could stop the whole thing if I wanted to."

I drank several fast swallows of wine. "Why don't you?"

"I guess I think let them have him. That old man experience."

I laughed, and she looked shocked by my laughter.

"They're like hummingbirds," she said. "Adept, agile, vicious."

"Is the hummingbird vicious?" I'd heard that before but I wanted her to repeat it.

"They wear acrylic nails. They yawn a lot. They take selfies."

"Jolie, why do you let him tell you these things? Why fill your head with it?"

"Oh, it keeps me company," she said.

The next morning, I went on a walk I used to take not with the ex I missed but by myself, through the neighborhoods where professors lived in unkempt family splendor—orphaned shoes and unraked leaves, sidewalk chalk and lacrosse sticks—to a strange natural feature that had always puzzled me, a long, curving shelf of earth that angled upward from the ground in which white wooden doors were lined like broom closets. I'd wondered what was behind the doors: tins of Spam and moth-eaten blankets? Stores of supplies, I'd assumed, for an old-fashioned disaster, though I knew now that disaster was not behind us but was waiting for us impatiently. I approached a door and yanked on its handle. It didn't give. I yanked again. What a glistening, glittering day it was, the colors so bright they hurt. I wish I could say I banged on the door, kicked it, railed against its unyieldingness, but I was not prone to dramatic gestures. I wish I could say in the face of that closed door I recognized that I was not meant to find what I was looking for. Instead, I kept walking to Elliewood Avenue, where there was a bookstore I'd liked. A Saint Bernard used to sprawl across the floor, and I'd step over his big, warm, slowly breathing body to get to the poetry section. It had amazed me, that there was so much poetry to be had and for so little, fifty cents, seventy-five. The books were riddled with marginalia, *water = forward march of time* or *There MUST be a new way to do consciousness*. I'd take them back to the town house I rented with Jolie, and read them in my room in my papasan chair, and I would feel something contained and peaceful move through me, the promise of the poems, yes, and also the suffering, the poet's suffering. For it was not my suffering, and I could look upon it benevolently, and be safe from it. It would find me eventually, but not there, not in that chair. Now the Saint Bernard was gone but the stuffed, musty shelves remained. I scuttled around contentedly for a while, finally settling on Renata Adler's *Pitch Dark*. It took the shaky-handed man (the original owner?) behind the cash register several tries to slip the book into a bag. And then, instead of giving me a bookmark, he handed me a hot-pink slip of paper advertising the store's going-out-of-business sale. "Tell me it's not so," I said, wagging it in the air.

"It's so," he said.

"I used to come here twenty years ago."

"You shouldn't have stopped."

I left the bookstore and walked quickly past an organic makeup emporium, a wine shop, and a boutique whose glass front displayed one exquisitely ripped pair of jeans. The town too had changed. You didn't just run into people anymore. If I wanted to see the ex I missed I would have to text him and tell him I was there, and we would meet and talk of polite things. There would be no clearing cloud, no truth revealed. Neither of us would say what we meant.

Maybe there *was* a thin thread that ran still between us—neither of us would acknowledge it. It was invisible in this world. Maybe it always had been, and when you were in love you could see the invisible, the symphony and understanding of the air, and when your love had ended you became consumed by the material world and could see only what was in front of your face. I walked until I found myself, by no conscious choice, approaching the town house where I'd lived, and I stood in front of it transfixed by three visions: in the first I lay in bed trying not to giggle as he pressed his mouth on me with a curious insistence rather than the light, flicking touch I desired; in the second I had already disappeared, chosen another man over him; and in the third I stood here now, looking back. I felt estranged from each vision, that I had not yet found my natural position, a time that would embrace me.

Jolie was in the kitchen when I returned to her house. "Don't you ever have to be at the hospital?" I asked, filling a glass with water from the refrigerator door.

"I'm on call," she said. "The broken bodies of Charlottesville are quiet tonight."

It wasn't night yet, but I didn't correct her.

"You know what scares me about Pat's women? Not what they know but what they don't know. When you're ignorant, you're dangerous. I worry they may hurt him. They have this intangible immense power over him. He makes fun of them because he's scared."

"How can you say that? He's so much older than they are," I said.

She shook her head. "You were always dating someone in college, and I envied you. But now I'm the one who's married. Now it's your turn to envy me! Because, in my heart, I'm not alone."

We made brownies from a mix, and as they were baking she did get called to the hospital. I took the pan out of the oven before they were done and ate an amorphous amount of chocolate ooze straight from it, and then I took a bath in Jolie's bathroom. The tile was a handsome pyramidical black and white but this room too had an air of abandonment. There were no bath salts or candles on the rim of the tub, no shampoo or conditioner in the silver holder. There was a bar of black soap. I let the hot water mute me, and then I got out of the tub and wrapped myself in a towel. I read in bed until very late that night. The next morning, Jolie still hadn't returned. I made coffee in her Chemex and drank it on her back porch, staring at the trees. Then I went back inside and wrote her a note. I told her that I couldn't say this to her face, but I thought she should divorce her husband. *It's not puritanism that makes me say so*, I wrote, *or the fact that he's taking advantage of you. It's just that I never liked him. I think you'd be happier alone.* I added a smiley face, scribbled the face out and spent the rest of the day wandering from empty room to empty room, catching views of myself in this or that surface, a mirror, a teakettle. Are *you* happy? I thought. I didn't leave the house. It rained a little. Yes, yes, I thought, I remember this. Jolie called that night as I was scrounging around for leftover pizza.

"It's such a clusterfuck here," she said. "Everyone's on vacation."

"Looks like I won't see you before I leave?" I was due to fly home the next day.

"Guess not. I'm sorry."

"Thanks so much for the hospitality," I said.

"That's another thing. Pat's women, they own one towel. One washcloth. They sleep in single beds. They have no concept of what it means to be with someone else."

"How can you be sure they even exist? He could be making them up."

"Why would he make them up?" she said.

"So you have something to talk about."

"What an awful thought! Well, you may be right."

The next morning, I packed my carry-on and summoned a Lyft and waited on the sidewalk in front of her house. My flight wasn't scheduled to leave for another five hours but I felt a building anxiety to be gone, a reckless impatience, and when the car pulled up to the curb with its windshield sticker and plastic lei dangling from the rearview mirror, my impatience turned to harrowing gratitude, as if I'd narrowly escaped an accident, as if Jolie's house was poised to explode, rise in a feathered ball of flames behind me. But when I slid into the back seat a jolt went through me: What if I'd forgotten to turn the burner off under the pot of water I'd boiled for my coffee and her house really did go up in flames? "I'm sorry," I said, "I have to run back in."

"No problem," the driver said.

I'd left the house key on the kitchen counter and locked the door from the inside, so I circled around to the back porch and cupped my hands to peer through the kitchen window. I couldn't see if the burner was on or not. I went back to the car. "You can go," I said. "Sorry again."

"Your bag," the driver said, popping the trunk.

And it was seeing the little gap open in the air between the blackness of the inside and the trunk door that changed my mind. "You know what? I'm coming after all." I closed the door and got into the car.

The driver grunted. "You got what you needed?"

"No."

"Nope," she said, and laughed. At the airport, I went through security and used the bathroom and pinned my hair back with a handful of bobby pins. I sat on a pleather chair and watched people stream past eating sloppy sandwiches out of paper bags and chattering into their phones. An electric cart drove down the concourse with two old women riding on the back, canes laid across the width of their side-by-side laps. I strained to remember what Jolie and I used to do together. Once we made black bean soup by pouring cans of beans into a pot and adding diced onion that we didn't think to sauté. We drank coffee at night at a café whose miniature glass salt and pepper shakers had enchanted me. We took the crumbs of life and squished them together to make a slice of bread. And then I did see him, not the ex I missed but the ex who missed me. He was carrying only a green backpack (he'd always traveled light), and was walking down the other side of the concourse, his lips fixed into a faint smile. I wondered what he was doing here—he lived in Columbus, where he was the director of a nonprofit that taught schoolchildren how to garden. He came closer and closer and turned and looked right at me and I opened my mouth to say something but he looked away. I got up from the chair and followed him, calling his name. He didn't turn around. Maybe he was distracted by the huge blue noses of planes nudged right up to the long wall of windows, or by anticipating whatever it was he'd come here to do. (I knew it wasn't to visit the ex I missed, for I had ruined their friendship.) He walked with his thumbs tucked under the straps of his backpack and his elbows jutted out like wings. I called his name again. The three visions I'd seen earlier had not shown me my future and I thought I saw it now in the faces of travelers bunched at gates, their agony and plain hope for wherever they were bound to go. He weaved and sprung among them, excuse me, excuse me, but I dropped the handle of my roller bag with a slap. And then something extraordinary. From out of the mass, the antsy mob that hummed with desire, a stranger reached down and grasped the handle. This is yours, he said as he thrust it toward me, and I was alone no longer.

Something in Common

The light here, when it's right, when it's not a smog-smudged gray, is extraordinarily beautiful, the long, wavery lines of the mountains like water stains on paper. I'm visiting my daughter where she lives near Los Angeles. She seems on edge around me, as if there's something broken in the next room and she really must see about it. She shows me my bed, square of sun as dense as tallow on its pillow, Ikea rug bright and striped at its foot. She opens the refrigerator and points to the Greek yogurts she bought for me for breakfast. "What do you have?" I ask, and she says she's just a coffee person. She used to eat stacks of toast slathered with cream cheese and jelly, rattling plates of Pop-Tarts. Her coffeemaker's an expensive, imported model that I can't comment on because she would take whatever I said as a criticism even if I didn't mean it that way. (I would mean it that way.) Coffee grounds are heaped darkly in a glass jar with a hinged blue lid. I think of her childhood's kitchen, the boxes of sugary cereal lined up on the refrigerator, the wet fart of its wrenched-open door.

In the backyard, we follow a rough stone path that circles a lime tree. I pride myself on knowing the names of things. The spiky bush with red blooms like tiny tubes of lipstick is an ocotillo, and there are ice plants in the garden bed rather than vegetables. Her bougain-villea is thin and wrinkly, but the crimson petals look pretty against the whitewashed wall of the garage. A neighbor's tree towers over her yard, rife with clusters of dry, brown, spear-tipped seeds. It's a female ash, and those seeds must drop and scatter and sprout miniature ash trees everywhere. She sees me staring. "It's the bane of my existence," she says, a placating thread in her voice. She wants something.

"Try putting down ground cover," I say. "Decomposed granite, wood chips."

"I could. I *should*." We complete the path's circuit and end up back on the patio. A little communion, to soften an oncoming blow. "You were always good with plants," she says.

"Not really—" I begin.

"Well, I'm off to work for a while."

"Are you?" I trail her forlornly into the house. She shoves her phone and laptop and a sweater into a brown canvas satchel, slips into sandals, and says she won't be long. The house is quiet after she's gone. What I was going to say was I just know a few things. Basic knowledge isn't so laudable but it's rare these days to know anything outside of one's pristine little sphere of brands and needs. I drag the throw from the couch into her bedroom and sit on her bed. She's thirty-seven and I'm sixty-six, newly retired from the library. I saw it there, saw how the young mothers, even in those addled, savage years, all had the same hairstyle, the same stroller, wore around their necks the same gold chain adorned with the dangling letters of their children's names. I saw how they'd created the same life for themselves, with minuscule variations. My daughter's room is very clean. The floor is swept, the walls are bare. A scrap of paper on her nightstand says *boy thinks balloon = mom so what does that look like? scary? silly?* She's a children's book illustrator, and I suppose this is a note for a drawing. The jewelry box I gave her two birthdays ago is nowhere to be seen. Instead, her necklaces and bracelets and earrings are artfully arrayed on a black enamel tray. She has particular taste—still, I thought the jewelry box was pretty, with its bright drawers and hammered tin door. I lie down on top of her comforter, seething a little with the feeling that I've been dealt an unfairness. But there's a nice breeze coming through the window, and I fall asleep.

I'm woken a short time later by the scrape of mail going into the mailbox. It's just as well. I brush my teeth with my daughter's toothbrush and wave it in the air to dry the bristles, riffle through her medicine cabinet until I find a jar of moisturizing cream. Uncapped, I see the place where her index finger's gone, like a swipe into cake icing. I'm here to house hunt. She doesn't know it. Earlier, when we drove in, we passed an open house at a little white adobe around the block, and I decide I'll go see it. If she were here, I wouldn't, I'd deem it too soon, too close. But she's left me alone. I rub the cream under my eyes and onto my neck, and walk around the block.

The house is marked by a cluster of yellow streamers fashioned into a puffy bow that tops the *For Sale* sign. A man comes out of the house next door and hoists himself into an enormous van whose windows are covered with paper blinds. As he drives away I picture a handful of jacks and a red rubber ball rolling and skittering across the floor, getting stuck under seats until the van takes a corner too quickly and then skittering out again, dust-covered. If I were the realtor I'd have asked him to park it elsewhere.

Inside the house, the floorboards are painted white. The bricks of the fireplace are painted white. The tiny kitchen has white counters and a white enamel sink. There are two small bedrooms and one bathroom with black-and-white tiles in a pyramidical pattern. The realtor lets me look unimpeded. The possibilities are limited, just as I want. I make an offer for more than it's worth.

"Why would you move here?" my daughter asks with more equanimity, I have to admit, than I'd anticipated. Still, the question stings.

"For you." I add, "And the weather."

"Your life's in Reston."

"Used to be, true, but not anymore. Monica moved to Michigan be closer to *her* daughter. Terri's children are begging her to do the same."

"Monica has grandchildren, so it makes sense. What will you do with yourself?"

I know well enough not to say *Speaking of grandchildren . . . !* She wouldn't need a partner, not with me around. She could go to a clinic, approach it sensibly, dispense with the mystery. What she doesn't understand is that I miss her youth, even if I sometimes seemed distant. The distance was protective. I had in some small way to stand apart from its happening, which was its ending. But it's not too late for her—I could take care of the baby and she could keep doing her illustrations, keep drawing pictures of balloons that boys think are their mothers and other mix-ups, confusions, satellites out to sea.

I return to Virginia and tell Terri that I'm moving to California. She takes me to breakfast and we order lattes. We order scones. There is no more pleasurable an activity a woman can undertake with another woman than eating a scone. Each time Terri takes a bite, she rubs her thumb and forefinger together to dust off buttery crumbs. What have I done? I think.

I move in early August. My daughter picks me up at the airport and we drive past palms with fronds like huge dusty feathers and the stucco facades of shops, Hubcap Annie's, Roadrunner Donuts. I see how the sun makes everything overt. Even what's ugly gleams a little, frank as a pulled tooth. We turn off the street we're on and drive for a few miles and turn again, and it's greener and quieter here, and then we're in a neighborhood I recognize. Soon we're pulling up in front of my new house. My daughter lets me in and we figure out how to get the air-conditioning going. There's an egg crate mattress and a sleeping bag on the floor. Sprinklers hiss on early the next morning. My daughter returns and drives me to Target and I pick out plates and cups and forks and spoons, a triple pack of toothpaste, toilet paper and a water bottle, a wicker laundry hamper. "You can always come back," she says, and I place a footbath into my cart. Its settings are *Massage*, *Swish*, and *Divine Swish*. The picture on the box shows water cast an unearthly shade of purple from the color of the plastic bath, a set of feet plunged into it as if into Easter egg dye. While not stout nor are the feet slim, and look as if they'd have to be wrenched out. Their stance indicates a stubbornness to be soothed, one I recognize. I mention that I'm having a hard time sleeping and my daughter loans me W. G. Sebald's *The Emigrants*. In Ambros Adelwarth's section, the narrator pauses before what he thinks is an empty house in a deserted resort town and sees a hand emerge from a window to shake out a duster "fearfully slowly," some pathos in the movement causing him to conclude that the town isn't empty at all, but occupied by women who do little more than move quietly and forlornly about.

I spread the book across my chest. When I was a young mother I did what I could to distract myself. We went into DC to the museums—which are free—most Sundays. We watched fireworks on the Mall on the Fourth of July. I made cube steak, carrot cake. I was like a sleeper caught not in a nightmare, nor in a dream, but in the lake-like middle where I swam through invisible water, and was tossed occasionally by some occurrence I couldn't ignore onto the shore.

The hand shaking out the duster *fearfully slowly*. I wasn't fearful, exactly, but in bringing about what I needed, I was slow.

The moving truck arrives. My daughter stands beside me as the men trundle boxes and furniture down the ramp. She admires a table lamp shaped like a clutch of tulips, one straight upward-rising stalk surrounded by three wilting stalks topped with blushing brown bulbs of glass. "It's yours," I say. The men pile the boxes high. I stare around me helplessly.

"One box at a time," my daughter says. She enjoys moving. She moved a lot before she ended up here, always with the promise of happiness in the next town, the next stop. Somewhere along the way she adopted a cat because she liked the way it sounded when he leapt to the floor, the soft, stuttered thumps of it. She told me this as if I should be enchanted by it, but the cat, named *Bird* in a fit of inspiration, ended up with me. I knew he would. He lived a good life and died from kidney failure at age nineteen. Now I'm the one who's chasing something while the object of my hopes stands beside me in jean shorts whose loose white threads dangle down her thighs and sift against her knees, opening the top flaps of cardboard boxes with her car key. She compliments my possessions as they emerge one by one, familiar to me but apparently less so to her, as if she didn't grow up in the same house with them, as if this pitcher painted with a bunch of grapes didn't hold her birthday party lemonade, as if this kitchen table wasn't covered with her sketch pads and pencils and chalks every single day. Maybe it's the surprise of seeing them in a new place. Maybe she forgives them that way.

I spot her in the grocery store, her head bent forward over a pyramid of peaches, her hair falling neatly over each shoulder. She looks up. "It's me," I say. We're separated only by piles of organic fruit.

"I know it's you," she says.

"You looked confused."

"It's funny, whenever I answer the phone you ask if I've been sleeping. I must sound confused too."

"Your voice doesn't have that false cheerfulness that so many people use on the phone."

"And my face doesn't have that look of alertness you expect in a face?"

"Not at this moment."

She laughs. "What are we going to do, me and you? I'm starting a new book. I'm getting into something."

"As you should be. Don't worry about me. I like being alone."

"I'm the one who likes being alone."

"Now we have something in common," I say.

Terri emails to ask if I'm settled in my new house. She says she's always wanted to visit Los Angeles, and to let her know when my guest room is up and running. I *think* you said you had a guest room? she writes. I reply that I'm not in LA, I'm about thirty miles east, but she should come visit anytime. An air mattress arrives from Amazon two days later, and then nothing. A week or so goes by and I email her to ask if the mattress is a sign that she's coming, or just a housewarming gift. Whenever it's convenient, sweetheart, she emails back. I think I know what's wrong. It didn't feel right to announce her intentions so baldly, and now she's being coy. She wants me to urge her, to coax her to visit. Normally I'd have no trouble doing so. But I've decided to start swimming and eat no meat and let myself tan a deep, pebbly tan, to buy an old Saab and pee with the bathroom door open and eat gelato straight from the carton and go to matinees and concerts in the park, take a blanket and spread it out on the grass and lie back and listen to children tromping around me, wailing with glee, and wonder what I did with my daughter all those years we lived together, how we understood each other, *if* we understood each other, if I scolded and lectured too much and didn't ever convey what I truly meant, if I had, by some fatal lack of tenderness, squandered the chance to shape her, to make her into an image in my mind, or if, worse, my mind was like the hailstone that had fallen once during a freak summer storm the year she turned eight, a strange, gray, clutched thing, not beautiful like a snowflake but a fist of cloudy ice *unable* to imagine, unable, in the way of objects, to know anything but itself, and I let tears snake out of my eyes and down my temples to wet my ears as I listen to the entertainment, the Misty Mountain Mamas, croon and shoulder-shake and play the banjo and tambourine. Which means I'm not going to wheedle for a visitor, I have other concerns.

My daughter calls to tell me that her illustrations for the book about the boy and the balloon have won an award.

"Congratulations!" I say. "What's the award?"

"It's from the National Association of Primary School Principals."

"I mean, is it money?"

"It gets a seal on its cover."

"A seal!" I say.

Silence on the other end.

"So, did you make the balloon scary or silly?" I ask.

"Really more absurd. Did I tell you I was considering making her scary?"

"It was on a piece of paper near your bed."

"What were you doing near my bed?" she says.

"Just straightening up. I don't remember exactly. Why do you sound so hostile?"

"I don't need you straightening up my bed."

"I didn't say straightening up your bed, I said . . . I don't know what I was doing. I feel like I'm on trial."

"I feel like *I'm* on trial," my daughter says. "For irreverence, or not being properly sanctimonious about mothers. Not portraying mothers as open arms of acceptance and grace."

"I don't expect you to portray me that way."

A pause. "She's not you."

"Who."

Her voice is urgent. "None of the mothers in my books are based on you, at all."

"Why should they be? I'm proud of you," I say. "You have talents I can't even dream of."

"But you don't entirely approve of how I put them to use."

I decide to be honest. "It's so much work, to make a drawing. Why not make a drawing that means something?"

She wears a pretty blue-and-white dotted dress to the award ceremony, thanking the presenter and speaking of the power of children perceiving adults as vulnerable sometimes, and how, when she illustrates a book, she feels that old power in herself. This doesn't sound right to me. Maybe she *did* see me and her father as vulnerable, but she never showed it. If she made this observation—that we were comic, ridiculous, corrupted by age—and derived comfort from it, she kept it to herself. She seemed, rather, terribly uncertain, and even more so after we divorced. We had been one and now we were two, and she didn't like the end of the illusion, seeing the horse costume come apart, her father the legs held up by suspenders, her mother the giant, braying head tucked under one arm. She seemed to grow mute before my eyes. Dinnertime was quiet. She did ask once if the divorce was her fault and of course I said no, but the question spoke to what I'd observed. I wished she were as confident as some of the other daughters of the mothers I knew, who laughed bawdily with each other and shared clothing and jewelry. I didn't realize at the time that all her doodling at the kitchen table was going to lead to anything—how could I? It so rarely does. And yet when I consider that in becoming an artist my daughter beat the odds, it doesn't register as a triumph to me but rather a kind of accommodation, an accommodation of that uncertainty.

After her speech, when I give her a hug I notice that she smells lightly, unobjectionably, of sweat. "I really am proud of you," I say, and she nods, yes, yes, and I leave her be so she can talk to the little throng that surrounds her. I wander over to a display that holds the book she illustrated, and one other award winner. Her book is called *Floating in Place*. I like the other book's title—*The Marvelous Way We Spent Our Day*—better, but I fight the urge to leaf through it, and open my daughter's book instead. Her illustrations are incredibly detailed. The boy's shirt is buttoned one-off, the cloth gullied with shadow like a shirt in a photograph. He's wearing folded-down high-tops and mismatched socks and a look of importunate curiosity on his face, and the balloon he thinks is his mother *is* absurd with her dried pasta hair and mouth open as if to yodel. I flip to the end to see what happens, for balloons have a habit of popping. The last drawing shows the boy in a room amid piles of toys, a flesh-and-blood woman standing next to him, and in the drape of her arm, in its careful curve that wants to pull and is wary of pulling the boy close I see something familiar, despite what my daughter said. If I still worked in the library I would slip the book from the shelf and prop it open on top.

I start toward her again but a man who's been lingering near the Brie and apricots beats me to it. He says something in her ear and she laughs. I make a quick exit.

I don't hear from her for a while after that, and then she invites me to dinner to meet him. She's made lasagna and he's made a salad and I've brought cannoli from Trader Joe's. Sometimes the world aligns into these perfect little unsullied moments of order. The table is set with linen napkins and shining plates and a flickering row of tea candles that spans its length, a shrine to the idea that beautiful objects make beautiful people, which, I realize, she's always believed and which her childhood did not embody. We cheers each other before we drink our wine. My daughter's pale-blue cloisonné bracelet slips down her arm. Her boyfriend's narrow shoulders are engulfed by a snap-button shirt with a flaunting Western scroll. I worry about her. She's so giddy she might crack.

Seeing her fall in love makes me lonely. You forget what a barricaded place love is until you watch someone enter it.

I break down and email Terri and urge her to visit. It turns out another friend of hers lives in LA, and she explains that it's not just me she's coming to see. Five days later, a car deposits her at the curb. It's good to see her. Her hair is cut into sweeping bangs and she's dispensed with or hid masterfully the bags beneath her eyes, the soft puckers of flesh that always reminded me of baby elbows. She admires the house. "It's like a sugar cube," she says. The friend in LA is actually her old college boyfriend, and he has a single friend who's new to the area too, and who'd like to meet me. "What do you think? A double date at Jacob's place?" she asks.

I agree reluctantly. The next night, we drive to Eagle Rock, where Jacob lives in a one-bedroom bungalow worth more than a million dollars. He's a short man with a stolid face like a stubborn rock. His friend, Bob, wears a jute fedora. We sit down to a dinner of stuffed tomatoes and zucchinis, a salad made with raisins and farro, fat wedges of lemon so juicy they explode when squeezed. Afterward I feel healthily satisfied enough to run a marathon, but instead we sit some more, in the living room now, drinking wine from bulbous wine glasses in which a generous pour appears but a few drops, talking about this and that. Bob says the way the film *The Favourite* was spelled with a *u* made him like it better, and I know exactly what he means. He says he's very easily influenced that way, very superficial, and I say that just because you have a gut reaction to something doesn't mean it's not a legitimate aesthetic preference, it's the softness of the *u*, the way with the *o* and *r* it spells *our*, the intimacy of it, as if the word has the same memories you have, and he says whoa, now I'm getting trippy, he just thinks it looks smart is all. But what does he know. What does he know. Speaking of memories—here he burps—last night he lay awake in bed unable to stop remembering the craziest thing he's ever done, which was bungee jump from the platform of a crane that stood over a harbor in Copenhagen. You dive straight down, he says, and in that instant you give up caring for anything you'd ever cared for in your life, and in its place you find the bulk and the grit of the wind. I turn to Terri to exchange a private glance, but Terri is no longer there.

Jacob's gone, too. "Why don't you come over here," Bob says.

He pats the couch cushion next to him, and I scoot closer. He lifts one of my legs and takes off my sandal and begins to kiss my ankle. It's a nice feeling, like I'm a library book being stamped.

The days of stamped library books! I appreciate, suddenly, how far into the future we've come.

"You're solid-boned," Bob says. His kisses move up my shin. "You've got a good, strong skeleton."

"What about you?" I murmur.

"Oh, I'm just a heap."

I raise my other leg and knee him in the jaw. He shakes his head, quickly, like a dog. "I'm so sorry," I say.

The hand cradling his jaw is gaudy with veins. He's kissing my other shin now, my knee, my thigh. I feel myself pulse, once, beneath my cotton underwear. When I was married, I missed a chance to have an affair with a fellow librarian who invited me to his hotel room at a conference. I sat on the floor of his room, drinking and talking, not holding his gaze long enough for either of us to figure out how to proceed. I prattled nervously and brayed with laughter, when, had I stilled, I might have felt the great quieting of desire come over me. I was stopped not by loyalty to my husband, for our marriage was almost over. I was stopped by picturing my body from the outside breaking through the air like panes of glass rather than from the inside where the darkness had tamped and softened it.

"We could go to my car," I say, and Bob raises his head, suddenly alert. His existence is a fact in the room, uncontested, while I'm poised on the brink of ridiculousness, slouched as I am with my heavy legs splayed across his lap. The door rattles and Terri comes back in. I scramble into a sitting position.

"Jacob's asleep," she announces, taking up my glass of wine and drinking from it. She must've carried hers to the bedroom with her. She sits with a contented *ah* on the armchair across from us and then seems to sense the room's halted quality. "Oh," she says, "did I interrupt something?"

We rush over each other to assure her that she did not.

She smiles. "If you say so." She pushes her bangs out of her eyes. "I'm not blind," she says. "I know Jacob's had a lot of women. It doesn't bother me. I don't resent him his life. One marriage, a quick divorce, a string of girlfriends. Whereas I was unhappily married for nearly forty years. I didn't have sex for the last twenty of them. I forgot what sex was, I think."

"Fault him," I say.

"What?"

"You don't fault him his life." I get up.

"Where are you going?" Terri turns to Bob quickly, with a sort of animal instinct. "What's your number?" She retrieves her phone from her purse. "You two should exchange numbers," she says.

"We'll connect again through Jacob, won't we?" he says.

"I doubt it," I say. "It was nice to meet you."

"Well." He stands up, looks uneasy. "I think that's pessimistic. How about"—his eyes roll Terri's way, wanting her to do the severing work for him. He *is* quite large, with a chin that quivers like pudding.

I make my way out to the car and lean on the horn until Terri comes running, clutching our sandals by their back straps.

The Saab starts rattling wildly on the 210. I take the next exit and get us to a gas station. The garage is closed, but the guy in the convenience mart says to leave the car and someone will look at it in the morning. I call my daughter for a ride home.

"I haven't seen her in how many years?" Terri asks as we sit on the curb waiting for her.

Neither of us can remember. When my daughter arrives she gets out of the car and gives Terri a hug and relief courses through me, and I realize I thought she was going to greet her from behind the window. "You look beautiful!" Terri cries.

"You do too," my daughter says. "And you, Mom."

I reach out and take her hands, which turn in my grasp but I hold on, I squeeze hard until they still. What she doesn't understand is it doesn't matter anymore, it stopped mattering at least an hour ago. I clung to it for too long, I admit.

Terri and I settle into a nice routine of watching a late-morning, extravagantly long movie (Julie Christie's jawline in *Doctor Zhivago*, its agonizing perfection!) that renders us woozy and weak when it's over, reluctant to restore ourselves to the grinding brightness outside the drawn blinds. We steep in the movie's aftereffects and then we go for a walk past my daughter's house. There's almost always another car parked in the driveway, pulled up right behind hers. "Should I knock?" I ask.

"Let her be," Terri says.

A week later, I drive Terri to the airport. I'm filled with a swell of nostalgia. "You've been a good friend," I say.

"Oh, shush," she says, and gives me a hug, and I watch as she disappears through the automatic doors, and continue to watch as people come and go, the banal emergencies of their faces, until a policewoman waves me on.

At home, I deflate the air mattress and carry it into the garage.

That night I call my daughter. Her relationship is over, she says. It ended abruptly and she doesn't understand why. She asked but he couldn't explain. He said they'd never figured out what to do together, and when she tried to, to just *touch* him for a moment, to wrap her hand around his wrist gently and with this simple gesture remind him of what they had, he said he was starting to feel trapped. Then he left. It would've been better if he'd seemed sad or regretful, but he was so decisive about it, she says. Actually, it would've been better if she didn't like him so much. I exhale as if I've been punched. No, no, I say, it's going to be all right. I'm rushing. Someone else is out there, I say, and you could meet him tomorrow or you could meet him in ten years. The only thing that stands between you is time, and time is built to be traversed. Look at me. I was so far away from you. Now I'm here.

Shifting Occupancies

They treated themselves at the end of each year with a trip to the desert. There was something unfailingly optimistic about the long, light sky, and by the time they arrived in Desert Hot Springs at a hotel with three naturally heated springs on its property, they were both in high spirits. Seth would drive on to Joshua Tree, where he'd rented a little house, but first he helped Laurel carry her bags into the lobby, introducing himself to the woman behind the desk as her driver. They kissed goodbye. "Nice driver," the woman said.

"Oh, that was my husband," Laurel said, laughing. She could afford to be frivolous with this woman, this pleasant helper in peacock feather earrings who was not the manager of the hotel. Laurel could just make out the manager standing at a worktable in the back, using a curved knife to cut a block of green glycerin soap into cakes for the rooms. This was her third visit, and the manager would not let on whether she remembered her or not.

The helper led her out of the lobby, across the patio, and to her room. All of the rooms opened onto the patio. White linen curtains hung from a line strung inside the double glass doors. There was a platform bed and a concrete floor. The room was cold. The cold was sharper in the desert than in the San Gabriel Valley. The mountains weren't smog-shrouded but enormously visible, their sides scored with long crisp folds, runnels through which snowmelt flowed, and the cold, too, felt clearer, more significant. She plugged in the electric heater, rolled it as close to the bed as she could get it, and texted Seth to see how he was faring. He replied that the house was heated only by a pellet stove. *I'm freezing my balls off*, he wrote.

Ah, but this was good for them, wasn't it? Getting away from their lives, getting away from each other. On a wooden shelf was a laminated menu of massages one might order (the manager was the masseuse; it was generally understood that she was not trained). *Just-What-You-Need; Couples-Just-What-You-Need; Deep Deep (Really Get Into Those Troublesome Parts); A Sensory Trip For The Mind And Body And (Maybe Even) Spirit.* The idea of engaging the manager to massage her was a horrifying breach of the manager's mystery. No, she was here for the springs, three concrete pools heated by the geothermal wells the town was known for. She changed into her suit, and with a towel and novel tucked under her arm she went to submerge herself in the warm pool. A wind picked up, raking the palms and sending a wren spinning off into the sky and a shiver of delicious contentment though her.

She sank into water to her chin, flexed her calves and wiggled her feet. From her place in the pool she could see the building that enclosed the hottest of the springs mere steps across the patio. The building was twelve-sided, with wooden walls and a corrugated metal roof that angled upward toward a hole cut into the middle to let out steam. This was the prize, something to admire from afar, to anticipate its enclosing warmth, the steam that rose from the water's surface and the hollow slap and gurgle of the water as it swayed into and out of the pipe that fed it. The wind gusted once again. She climbed out of the water, hurried to the twelve-sided building, and wrenched open the glass door only to discover that someone was in the pool already. A couple could be ignored, but another solo soaker had to be acknowledged. She dropped her towel gamely. "Just need a little warm-up," she said.

"Of course." The skin above the man's upper lip was beaded with water, as if he wore a sparkling mustache. Laurel made a show of reading her book as they sat in silence in the haze and heat, but she couldn't concentrate with him there—it felt unnatural to read in a stranger's presence, and she had to hold the book at an awkwardly high angle to keep it out of the water. When she marked her place with the dust jacket and looked up, he was staring at her frankly. "How is it?" he asked.

Laurel liked it so far, but her tastes had changed. She used to read as a writer does. Now all she wanted was for the story to pick her up and carry her along and deposit her somewhere else, unaware of how she'd gotten there. The characters in the novels she read spoke to her like her friends did, regaled her with their suffering for which she truly did feel sympathy tinged with tawdriness, a voyeur's pleasure in their misfortune. It wasn't the misfortune she experienced as pleasure, it was the distance she stood from it. For the last eight years, as she'd followed Seth from teaching job to teaching job, she had been writing a novel. But it was a heavy, tethered form, and it dragged her down and held her under and she sensed with the thrumming attunement animals brought to their environment a shining place above her, and she stopped working on it and came up. The shining place wasn't visible once you were in it, surrounded by it.

She knew her friends must feel sorry for her. They must say what they were supposed to say, Laurel got so busy with her job. What *is* her job? some must ask and others answer, She's a copywriter, isn't she? Yeah, I think she's a copywriter.

They would not understand that only when you stopped wanting, stopped grasping, did the gift give itself to you.

Time, as sweet and dense as honeycomb.

Now she replied to the man's question about whether she liked the novel she'd placed a careful arm's length away. "I don't know yet. I'll tell you when I'm a little farther in."

～

The pellet stove didn't feel like it was putting out much heat. Seth had just finished unpacking groceries—coffee, half-and-half, pasta, tomato sauce, bagged salad, wine—when he heard Juliette's car in the dirt driveway and went out front to greet her because this would be the last time, though she didn't know it. She stepped out of her car and dropped her bag at her feet and opened her arms. She would expect him to rush to her and pick her up and carry her into the house. Which he did, knocking her head against the doorway when he pivoted to enter. He apologized. He knew she was starting to hum inside like a windup toy and indeed she leaned her body in his arms to steer him toward what she guessed, correctly, was the bedroom. Seth was thirty-eight. She wouldn't let him forget that he was ten years younger than her. "Can you just be a fucking feminist for once and stop nattering about it," he'd said during their sole fight, and to his surprise she laughed at him.

He dumped her onto the bed and she bounced neatly back up to a sitting position. Her hands found his belt buckle.

"Can I get you something to drink?" he said.

"You sound like a stewardess. You can—" and she described a sexual endeavoring with such specificity he felt the embers of arousal in his stomach snuff out. The lingua franca among women in their forties was that they would inhabit and delight in themselves as they wished they had when they were younger, so Juliette inhabited and delighted in herself, speaking brashly of her body and its pleasures and needs. She cast off her shirt and hoisted her breasts out of her bra. Her nipples were like the soft eyes of a drunk. He had to tell her they couldn't see each other anymore. He would not say he hoped they'd remain friends because he knew they would not remain friends. And because they would not remain friends, he had to wait until the last day of the trip to do so.

They had started out as friends. She was the director of communications for the college where he taught history. She was always going on terrible internet dates, and they'd have lunch and she'd tell him about them. "You never talk about Laurel," she said one day. She knew Laurel a little—they saw each other occasionally at events at the college.

"There aren't as many adventures attached to that subject," he said, which was harsher than he meant to be. He was trying to compare a marriage of eight years, the stories he could squeeze out of it, to Juliette's tumultuous flings. But she seemed pleased with his answer, seemed to think he was flirting.

"I'm an adventure to you, am I?"

Seth laughed. "Yeah, you'd be an adventure." It was funny that he was flirting back with this person he wasn't at all attracted to, he thought, before realizing that he was, just this moment he was, less attraction than a swift shifting force inside him that unfolded itself in his chest like a pair of massive wings. The span of it shocked him. Later that day he texted Laurel to say that he'd forgotten there was a talk he had to stick around for, and she texted back an emoji of a face wearing a knowing smile. It seemed to say *I'll withhold judgment, mister, but whatever you're doing is probably unnecessary.* What he was doing was having sex with Juliette on her couch. To be caught between an urgency that built until he was sure there was nothing but its detonation and bright fallout in which he lost himself, his contours and earthliness, and then the process of return as he took on weight and shape again—in other words, metamorphosis—yes, maybe that wasn't *strictly* necessary. His confusion might've turned to fatal regret had Juliette—naked and wiry as a dancing skeleton—

not fetched a bottle of scotch and two glasses. They drank. She sat back and spread her legs like a man on a subway, and he crouched in front of her, knowing this proved his respect, how equitable he was in terms of ministering pleasure. She began to laugh and pushed his head away.

Now he got up from the bed in the rented house and pulled on his jeans. "Let's go on a hike," he said. The park was nearby, the Joshua trees furry and listing.

❧

Laurel was walking along the hotel road, a luminous, jellied quality to the air. Morning, not quite seven o'clock, the distant white wind turbines like wavy lines of crosses planted at the feet of the mountains. A medical glove star-fished in the scrub. Blossoms on cacti like crepe-paper thumbprints. She never walked far, just up and down the road a few times. Back in the lobby, she spotted the man from the pool in the kitchen where coffee and breakfast were laid out. He was wrapped in a robe, cutting a piece of Meyer lemon cake. She'd intended to pour herself a cup of coffee but at the sight of him she continued out the door that led to the patio. She had a habit of avoiding men who made her feel this way, this prick and skitter of awareness. Before Seth the avoidance had a textured, erotic quality. She ignored those whom she knew she would come to love. And then put off saying so, waiting for a moment of unimpeachable integrity until it became a mind game, for what did one mean when one said I love you, and how could one know for sure at their tender age, and who would be crass enough, brave enough, crazy enough to say it first, and how would that person broach it, and would that person cry, and would that person look beautiful crying, and so forth. Now that she was married the avoidance couldn't give. There was no crumbling of will to look forward to, no slow descent into the softness of begin-nings. She turned away.

Not that she felt, with this man at the hotel, that there was any-thing to avoid except speculation. It was all on her side, she was sure.

After she'd had her coffee and fruit and toast slathered with Nutella, she swam laps in the cool pool, soaked in the warm pool, and entered the twelve-sided building where he was installed again. Apparently it couldn't be avoided—when one person spent so much time in one particular pool, it might seem as if he was always being interrupted when in fact he was the interrupter, ignoring the natu-ral flow of the place, the gently shifting occupancies.

She gave herself permission not to apologize as she joined him, and he said in a conspiratorial voice as she sank into the water, "Feel nice?" and Laurel realized her face must be dumb with pleasure.

She blushed. She didn't want to play along, didn't want to ad-mire his angled collarbones and lean shoulders and blithely revealed interest.

"That book I was reading?" she said. "I do recommend it."

"What was the title?"

She named the name of the novel that was a novel in name only.

"Thanks." He yawned. It turned out that he was an actor. He used to do theater exclusively, but you couldn't make a living doing that, he said. Now he did television. Television was easy money, just very limited people with large heads reciting lines some twenty-six-year-old Iowa grad had written. "Not to be gratuitous about it but I could write that shit! I could but I wouldn't."

He told her about a few of the plays he'd done. "So this may in-terest you. I did *Shoppers Carried by Escalators into the Flames* a while back. Denis Johnson. It was in New York, at the Dimson. I got to talk to him a little and I'll never forget what he said about himself. How he described himself. He said, and I quote, he was a 'criminal hedonist turned citizen of life.'"

She didn't reply for a moment. "I guess I find that strangely impersonal. Like it's a process he's describing, something outside himself."

"Really?" he said. "I see it as turning from estrangement—I suppose that's being outside yourself—to a radical intimacy."

"How intimate is it to be a citizen of life, though?"

"Life's a big thing. Most people don't feel they have access to it. He was saying that he was staking a claim."

Then he asked her what she did, and she said she was a freelancer, and he asked her what type, and she said the writer type, and he asked her what sorts of publications she wrote for, and she said alumni magazines, law firm blogs, the occasional professional association quarterly, making sure to maintain a hearty note of contentment in her voice. She was getting hot and rose to leave. He didn't follow her.

~

Juliette shuffled around the kitchen as they made dinner, her socked feet thrust into Seth's wool slippers. She said their relationship had become about more than the sex, of course.

"What do you mean of course?" he said.

"It was its basis and it's not anymore. We didn't get together to talk about Robespierre."

"Why, is it bad?"

Her face cracked open with pity and triumph. "No! That's not what I'm saying but your worry is touching."

"I'm not worried. Funny you would interpret that as worry."

"Funny? What else could it be?"

"Ever heard of pure curiosity?"

"The cologne for intellectuals?"

He didn't laugh. He dumped the pasta into a colander, steam clouding his glasses.

"Speaking of curiosity, how often do you and Laurel have sex? I bet not as much as you used to. Same with us, but if anything I feel closer to you."

It was unseemly of her to bring Laurel into it, though he knew it wasn't really about Laurel. And he didn't agree that they had sex less—it seemed nearly incessant, like a roller coaster that had no line so you rode it again and again, the front car this time, the back the next, the place where you knew your picture would be taken so you mimed pleasure with overly large gestures . . .

He felt weak, suddenly, and sat at the table under a sign that read *Bless the Food Before Us and the Love Between Us* and wondered if love, unbound, invisible, would really content itself ponging back and forth during some lame couple's dinner. He doubted it.

Juliette poured the pasta back into the pot and mixed it with tomato sauce and veggie sausage sautéed with onions and peppers. Why had it come to his eating an early dinner in a freezing house with a woman who was not his wife? Yes, he was going to end things, but the affair would remain immutable. Maybe Laurel would never find out. Maybe she would. That wouldn't change the fact of its happening, only whether it was received, rued, discussed, whether it hardened and grew into the blade that severed his marriage. He had not thought through this possible severing. Had he acted out of spite? No. Boredom? Not really. Think, he told himself. Examine your life. It was too disheartening to admit that there had been no good reason, that he had been acting on chemical impulse, his body no better than a circuit box, fuses connecting simply and mechanically and at the behest of nearly anyone who stopped before him. Actually, it had been his ego Juliette had appealed to. The ego tripped the body, it happened that way.

And yet there was an element in his marriage to Laurel of being held back, of an expanding circle of energy sucked back into incipience. Their routine was limiting. He knew Laurel must feel it, too,

but some arrogance inside him ardently believed it was his unique-
ness being snuffed out, not hers. His potential for being whoever
he would've been without her. He thought of this person every so
often with a tenderness he could not summon for himself.

Juliette was speaking. ". . . if we drove home, we could stay at
your place for once."

Seth shook his head. "The neighbors."

"I have neighbors too."

"And I'd basically have to turn around and drive right back out
to get Laurel."

"If we left now we'd be home in two hours. We'd have two nights
with central heating."

"I like it here." He speared some pasta. "But Juliette, if you're that
cold, you should go. There's no reason you should stay and suffer."

"We could keep each other warm," she said, pushing her bowl away.

"Juliette."

"Stop saying my name."

"I'm sorry."

"Are we ending things, is that it?"

He felt a rush of relief, then annoyance that she'd beaten him to
it. "I need to."

She shrugged. "There's really nothing to end."

"This is nothing? I guess it's true you risked nothing. I didn't."

She took his hand and turned it over and kissed the inside of his
wrist. Humiliatingly, he blinked back tears.

❧

She was in the lobby reading the newspaper when the manager
emerged from the recesses beyond the front desk carrying a fresh
lemon cake. She made them dense and bitter, with a sticky, tangy
glaze. "Warm enough?" she asked, proceeding into the kitchen.

"I am now," Laurel called. "Thanks."

"I see you've been enjoying the springs."

"I love swimming, I love heat, I love solitude." What else do you love? she thought. Buttercups?

"But don't you feel," the manager said as she reemerged, "that one experiences solitude most precisely in the company of others?"

"I lose myself with others."

Cinnamon toast, melancholic piano riffs?

"I'm the person in a group always listening, asking questions," Laurel continued. "It's with women, what I'm describing. I'm very submissive with women."

The manager rested her hand on the back of Laurel's chair. "What do you need to be submissive about?"

"The fact of being another woman, I guess."

She wondered what would happen if she took her hand in her own and said tell me how to be, if the manager had been waiting with perfect patience to anoint her new acolyte and with that question Laurel would ascend. Instead she returned to her room and texted Seth to ask if he was getting much writing done.

Sadly no, he replied.

Why not? she wrote.

Ellipses danced on her screen.

⌁

Robot writing fingers failing. All is discord, he texted.

"What'd she want?" Juliette said.

"Nothing."

"Did you tell her you're hers again, only hers?"

He had a quick, threadbare impulse to jab Juliette with his elbow. "You know what? I'm leaving too."

"I thought you liked it here," she said.

"I do. But I'm married."

"It's funny, you men, you take everything too seriously. You take yourselves too seriously, that's why."

They packed in silence, and Seth closed up the house. He stripped the sheets and left them in a lump on the floor, shut the lid of the pellet stove, placed the key in a basket on the kitchen counter, and locked the door behind him. Though he did not mean to, he pulled out of the driveway right behind Juliette and followed her car all the way home. He couldn't bring himself to pass her. They reached Claremont in an hour and a half. He felt a little pang when she turned off the street they were on to the street that led to her neighborhood. She did not honk like he hoped she might.

When he let himself in at home, he half-expected to see Laurel there, but of course she was in Desert Hot Springs, where he would have to return to fetch her the day after tomorrow. He walked to the bedroom, lay down on her side of the bed, and pressed his face to her pillow. A vision of her came to him, her head thrown back in laughter. Imagine this, she said, thrusting the *Courier* into his lap. It was open to an obituary. *Meredith Hickey née Caruso*, it read. Imagine making that decision, she said. Willingly becoming a Hickey. She looked lovely laughing, unaware of herself, and he thought if only she could've always been unaware of herself what a beautiful woman she'd be. Then the vision flipped up its tail like a cellophane fortune-telling fish and her face betrayed that crucial self-consciousness that was beauty's enemy. Laurel with her deadlines and licorice bridge mix, Laurel with her novels and oversized sleep T-shirts, Laurel with old aspirations he could hardly name. To do a different kind of writing. To live a different kind of life. Maybe he'd put them out of his mind to save her feeling like he was tracking her failure, or maybe it was his feeling for her, in which case he couldn't fess up to it, wasn't supposed to have it. Who was she, to occupy disappointment so easily?

~

The actor had turned on the timer to activate the jets and the water roiled and swirled, white froth icing the surface, bubbles clinging to his arms. She went in and under, where she was buffeted by sound like a diced carrot in a pot of boiling soup, and came up gasping.

"You'll explode," he said.

"I know." She was smiling. She would be friendly, she decided. It was okay. She and Seth had gotten married at city hall. A few months later they threw a party at which Laurel didn't drink because she was newly pregnant. The thought that she was pregnant—that was where life began. But she had a miscarriage and six years later she got pregnant again and had an abortion. She did it right away. Seth agreed.

The actor drifted as if propelled by the turbulent water closer and closer until she could feel his leg against hers, the silky slip of his skin. "Are you okay with this?" he asked. The jets shut off and she straddled him and they looked at each other and laughed. With one hand he undid the drawstring of his trunks and with the other plucked aside her suit. The water was clear again, as if they sat in the belly of a magnifying glass, and he pulled her onto him and she remembered how last year she and Seth had ridden in an aerial tram to the top of Mount San Jacinto. The glass car stopped halfway up and swayed back and forth, the engine heaving against its bulk. They were so exposed! The climb was two and a half miles and only as it happened was it possible—the second it stopped the mechanical world stopped too and they hung among the elements, the raw parts of nature, sky, sun, mountain, cloud, which appeared through the rounded windows as figures of emotion rather than matter if only they could break through to them and live among them properly, without distance. But they were not natural beings, they dangled in midair, gawking at the obdurate blueness. She placed her hands on the actor's shoulders and leaned in close. His breath was puffing into the hollow of her throat. She let elation drain through her.

~

He threw himself into his writing, first with coffee and then with a small glass of aquavit. It all came back to him, Robespierre and the Feast of the Supreme Being, descending a papier-mâché mountain in a toga, Trump's ride down his golden escalator, Sam Nunberg saying *We could have had women in bikinis, elephants and clowns there. . . . It would have been the most gloriously disgusting event you've ever seen.* False deities come to earth to govern by persuasion, cruelty, farce, force. He needed to work this out. Why hadn't he worked this out in Joshua Tree? Fucking really wasn't that rarefied an activity. He wished Laurel would text again to ask how the writing was going so he could say it was going, at least, and he was sorry he'd been flippant with her earlier, and tomorrow they'd stop for a date shake on their way home.

~

She was returning her dirty breakfast dishes to the trolley outside the kitchen window when she saw, in a room whose doors were wide open, the manager giving the actor a massage. She had avoided knowing which room was his but now she came closer and there he was, dressed in cloth shorts, lying on a folding table on his stomach while the manager chopped at his back with the sides of her hands. She said something and he turned over and she kneaded his calves and feet. His head lolled.

"You can come in," the manager said.

She entered the room and went to stand beside him. His eyes were closed, his eyelashes like black threads.

"You can touch him if you want."

"I'm not going to touch him."

The manager's kneading slowed and then stopped. "You eat with your eyes only?" she said.

Again she remembered the view of the Coachella Valley from the tram. According to the brochure she was given when Seth bought their tickets, the palms that grew on the valley floor were surrounded by a system of sand dunes that lizards swam through to escape from predators. The lizards had shovel-shaped jaws, and scales on their feet to give them traction. Still they were being crushed by the tires of off-road vehicles. She fished the brochure from her pocket and opened it for Seth at the top of the mountain. She enlisted his sympathy.

Falconer

Soon the first cars will arrive for mass. I can picture them floating down the streets of our city, this suburb of Los Angeles populated by gladsome old people and families with small children and a
murky middle swath to which my husband and I belong. I'm idling
at the curb of Our Lady of the Assumption while my son and his
friends butt a white plastic parking barrier into the hatchback, turning it this way and that, trying to make it fit. I wish they'd taken it
from the extras stacked near the parking lot's chain-link fence. To
take from the extras is more like thrift, less like theft. To put an un-
used thing to use is nearly to be a liberator of the unloved. But they
did not take it from the extras, they took it from the middle of a
row bisecting the lot into pickup and drop-off zones. On its side, it
resembles a toddler's stubby slide. Adrian reaches through the open
back door and slaps around near the headrest, and the seat flops flat.

"Bro finally," Victor says. They get the barrier in and then Victor
sits on Emilio's lap and Adrian rides shotgun. I pull away and make a
quick U-turn, and when we reach Mountain Avenue there's a burst
of relieved laughter.

"You know that kid Falconer?" Emilio says. "Me and Robby were in the four hundred quad before third period and we saw the police take him out of class."

I stifle the urge to say Robby and *I*. Instead I ask, "Neil?"

"Yeah," Adrian says, and I can tell he doesn't want me to say more.

We arrive at the skate park and they unload the barrier and carry it to where the lip of the shallow bowl meets the flat ground. Adrian empties the water from his bottle into the base of the barrier, then uses the bottle to ferry water from the drinking fountain to the barrier again and again. He looks so much more industrious than he does at home. At home he carries himself like someone arriving late to a movie unperturbed by what he's missed, nonchalant about the storyline, he's heard it all before, the words my husband and I are going to say, the arguments we're going to make for literature, the impassioned pleas—in three, two, one—we're going to lodge on its behalf. Sometimes the spectacle of belief is enough to turn you off to it. But he humors us and reads what we put in front of him (and we have to, for his English teacher, nostalgia-crazed, teaches only Dylan lyrics). He reads *The Great Gatsby* and *Jesus' Son* and *This Boy's Life* and Cortázar's "Axolotl," man meets salamander story—"And then I discovered its eyes . . . lacking any life but looking, letting themselves be penetrated by my look, which seemed to travel past the golden level and lose itself in a diaphanous interior mystery"—and speaks insightfully about what he's read immediately afterward and never again. And so the question for those of us who put stock in such things, who lamely make too much of them, becomes, Where did it go? That mystery? That mystery that weighs inside you as if it's your own thumb on the scale?

Emilio produces a roll of duct tape from his backpack and they crouch around the barrier—I can't see what they're doing—then stand and get on their boards and roll up to it tentatively at first, up and away, pivoting at the hips in their dark clothing, sharp sound of wheels coming down. Crow-like, their pecking. And in a gust they're rolling up to the barrier with more speed, they're clearing it.

Neil Falconer and Adrian were inseparable for a year, from the summer before seventh grade to the summer before eighth. They lived on opposite sides of a park, our house on a dead-end street to its north, Neil's low-slung duplex to its south. Sidewalks streaked with runoff from profligate watering. Smog-blurred mountains, their craggy snouts glazed with sugar icing. That first summer, Neil would knock on our kitchen door at eight o'clock in the morning carrying a crackling bag of Takis he'd skated to Walmart to buy. Adrian would be eating breakfast, and Neil would ask him if he could have a yogurt or a banana. I'd learned not to offer him anything. There wasn't a mother in the picture. There was a father, a sister. Once I drove him to the post office so he could get a check for his father from a PO box. His father did home inspections, Neil said. Their car was in the shop, Neil said. His lies made me love him.

He had bulbous eyes and milky legs and the freedom that anonymity bestowed upon the anonymous. I wondered how our house struck him, with the platter of fruit on the kitchen counter and the glass jars of granola and almonds and walnuts. The Bialetti on the burner, the framed illustration of birds' eggs—dangling planets mottled blue and caramel and gold and surrounded by coiling umbilical-like ribbons—over the stove. In the refrigerator, the Greek yogurts he liked. Our house was modest, a stucco cube with three small bedrooms, a galley kitchen, and a sprawl of electric-pink bougainvillea staked to the whitewashed wall of the garage. My husband and I didn't teach over the summer, and my husband was often on the couch with his laptop or a book while I wandered from room to room. Gathering up glasses. Rinsing them in the sink. I could repeat a small gesture infinitely.

One morning that summer, I watched Neil and Adrian through the kitchen window skating the larger of the two ramps that my husband and Adrian had built in the driveway. They balanced on the lip, back wheels down, front raised. Their shoes were ripped, their laces knotted like lengths of popcorn string. The *ka-thunk ka-thunk* as they rolled from Masonite to metal to concrete. They wove around the car on their way to the street, which slowed them down, a good thing, as softball parents in their trucks (beds glossily lidded like coffins) might miss a kid shooting out of a driveway. (There had been trouble, recently, with softball parents. Drunken softball moms arguing in front of the house after softball prom. A limousine idling, and our Hillary sign tossed into the succulents.)

After a while they came inside and rummaged in the bureau for tea candles. "I dreamed last night where I did a backside tailslide down the rail of the five-stair," Adrian said.

"You should've tried it on the eleven-stair. *And then*"—Neil raised his voice over Adrian's objections—"backside big-flip out." They popped the candles out of their tin pans and went back outside, and I moved to the front bedroom and watched them run the candles along the curb until it was dark with wax. Adrian attempted a boardslide before Neil was done waxing. The park lay on the other side of the street, grass strewn with rolling papers and condoms and fast-food wrappers stained with blots of grease. They tucked their boards under their arms and cut across the grass to the shuffleboard court, where they used a palm frond to sweep away the grass-skirt litter of other fronds and brought forth from the bushes an orange construction cone, a filing cabinet, and a long piece of wood that they wedged like a ramp between the pyramids of numbered tiles. (I took the dog out and crept close; they failed to notice.) They arranged the scavenged items carefully, the filing cabinet drawers in a kind of ziggurat, and rolled from one to another, nudging against, leaping over them. Their objective seemed simply to surmount things. Neil bent deeply at the knees, crossing and uncrossing his arms as he ollied into the air like a flung doll. Adrian rode upright, slower and less flamboyant and so quick off the ground you might miss him if you weren't watching closely. In Neil there was something unbidden, like a thought that came rushing to one's mind despite its inappropriateness, while Adrian was more cautious, withholding. When they were done skating they hid the obstacles in the bushes again. This went on for the next few weeks, one item exchanged for another—construction cone for milk crate, filing cabinet for desk chair whose casters wobbled like tops—until the landscapers who roared across the park on riding lawnmowers and rounded the bushes with whining weed eaters found their stash and hauled it away.

I wondered about that. If they did so reluctantly or with satisfaction. Burning villages to the ground.

Seventh grade began. Adrian and Neil weren't in the same classes, but they skated together after school and on weekends. They rolled the small ramp into the street using their skateboards as dollies. Sometimes other boys came by, their T-shirts a lacework of holes on the lower right where the grip tape rubbed when they carried their boards against their bodies. One boy offered himself up for sacrifice, lying on his back in the street, and the others on their skateboards began at the dead-end, the curve that nudged up against the edge of the park, skated with long pushes toward the prone body, leapt over it, landed, and rolled away hips canted so far forward it was as if they were being pulled from the navel by strings. An invisible hand might tug them, lift them into the air where they would backstroke haplessly.

They laughed and ragged each other. "Neil *Antonius* Falconer? Who named you, Caesar?"

Scrapes and blood were commonplace, but what would happen if one of them broke something? I guessed that their concern would be proportionate to their derision, but the hurt one would not permit it.

The weekend after the presidential election, Neil appeared as usual at our door. They were thirteen; I thought it my duty to give a speech. Adrian had heard me already—it was for Neil, my troubled words. He listened to me with a shy smile and when I had finished he said, "My dad says we have to accept it and make the best of it."

I walked the dog down his street, listening for tumult. The grass was thick and the windows shut and the garbage cans lined up in a neat row. I felt comfortable there. That spring, I saw Neil and his father at the park batting balls. Neil's father wore a knee brace and a mesh ball cap. He had low square shoulders and a red face and he stood on the pitcher's mound and red silt lifted and clouded about him. "Are you hesitant?" he called to Neil. "Watch me coming at you, plebe." I tugged the dog's leash. I knew he was an alcoholic, that he and Neil were extraordinarily close and yet he made the boy's life hell. I suspected he didn't approve of Neil skateboarding because he wanted him to play baseball, but maybe he sensed an overkind sentiment coming from me, tinged with self-regard. Those often privy to others' judgments develop a feeling for such things, and I'd prided myself on being accepting of Neil, knowing that some other mothers would not be. They would not shun him, but they would subtly make the friendship impossible. Their sons would become busy with piano lessons and soccer camps and trips to the Getty. Years ago, after my husband chaperoned Adrian's third-grade class on a field trip to the LA County Fair, he'd told me how Neil's father had ridden along on the school bus and it was unclear whether he was there as another chaperone or because he lacked transportation. On the way back he'd sat reading the newspaper unperturbed by the high-decibel ruckus taking place all around him, when suddenly he raised his head and hollered at a child who had reached across his seat to retrieve a wheel of Bubble Tape from another child, hollered with the great unfeeling vehemence of an auctioneer, then returned placidly to his paper.

I got the dog pointed in the opposite direction. I never looked Neil's way.

Not long after that I read in the *Courier* that Neil's sister had been sexually assaulted by a man who sold dates at the farmers market, a gaunt, cave-chested man with the scrabbling gaze of an insomniac. He was a "friend of the family," the article stated, and had gone to their apartment when Neil and his father weren't at home. I didn't think about the girl's fate, nor the dubious moniker "friend of the family," I thought only of whether to tell Adrian about what had happened, and decided not to.

Summer again. My husband made pickled shrimp served on a platter with paper-thin slices of lemon. We unfolded the Ping-Pong table. Neil didn't come around at first, and when he did he was on foot. He'd focused his board, he said. "I broke it on purpose," he said to me, and it struck me how neatly that word—*focused*—connected the quality of paying attention to an act of destruction. Adrian dug an old deck out from a stack in the garage and they took it to the skate shop and set it up with used wheels and hardware, and for a brief window of time it was the two of them again, skating down the street to the burred purr of wheels, and I felt something in my chest soften, turn to the pliant material of contentment. And then Neil disappeared again, and again emerged boardless. He'd left it at Uncle Sam's, he said, and Adrian went with him to an apartment where no adult ever seemed to be at home, and they microwaved chicken wings and watched anime.

Did he get it? I asked later, but he hadn't, and anyway what *it* was wasn't fixed, wasn't what I thought it was, was beyond my comprehension. One day Adrian came out and said it. "You repeat yourself," he said, and I did, I did. I stuttered over their closeness slipping away.

Eventually Neil stopped coming around entirely. By the time Adrian entered high school, he saw Neil not at all. Every now and then, with sudden passion, he'd say he missed him.

When he gets home from skating the Catholic parking barrier (that's how I think of it, stolid as a believer), I follow him to his bedroom. The inside of his door is papered with stickers, *Chocolate* and *Palace* and *Girl* and *Hockey* and a black bumper sticker whose white bubble letters read *My Kid Skates Better Than Your Honor Student*. I ask him why Neil was taken out of class by the police. There's no answer. "Adrian!" He removes an earbud, regards me dolefully.

"What?" he says.

"I was asking you about Neil. What happened?"

In a rush he says that a week ago Neil was at the skate park and someone gave him something, he couldn't tell what, and then last weekend Neil and Uncle Sam chloroformed a guy sitting in his car. Yeah, chloroformed. Yeah, no, it sounds crazy, saying it. Like a science experiment, like fleshy things floating in jars.

"*Neil* did?" I say. He nods. "And then what?"

Then they took the guy's wallet and phone, and someone called the police, and yesterday the police came to their school and took Neil out of class. He didn't see it. He's glad he didn't, he says.

The next morning, I use my phone to go to the church's website. There are masses all day long, from seven to six—Vietnamese mass, Spanish mass, English mass. We need to return the barrier, I tell Adrian.

"But people are skating it," he says. "We're filming clips on it." I've watched more than a few clips over Adrian's shoulder, hyper-intelligible slushy wheel sounds and pigeons rising from tide pools of fountain water and the light of foreign cities and the angles the skateboard makes apparent, angles of benches and railings and the sunken squares of municipal buildings, plazas whose black-tiled mosaics have gone soft and gray with dust. But clips aren't the point. The point is right and wrong. I have the feeling that Neil's paying for what we've done.

At six Adrian and I walk to the parking lot to scope it out. "I couldn't sleep last night," I say. "I kept having this image of myself getting up from the dinner table with greasy hands, fumbling a knife I was holding and stabbing myself in the stomach."

"Mom, you have a heartbreaking imagination," he says. We come to the middle school that shares the lot with the church. Clumps of long-stemmed lavender bushes. Parish Office. The lot is half-filled, the barriers indolently stacked. The back door of the church opens and a woman in a yellow silk jumpsuit emerges. She's holding a crying baby, jiggling the baby and whistling to it.

Adrian points to the bell tower. "We used to go up there. We threw the rope up so you can't ring the bell."

At the sound of Adrian's voice, the baby stops crying. The woman pivots so the baby can see him.

"He likes you," I say.

"He does!" the woman says. "He loves older kids and cement mixers and stuff."

"He did too," I say. "Remember those days?"

Adrian smiles and waves at the baby. "Kind of."

The barrier disappears from the skate park. What was stolen is stolen again. It has another life, maybe. Three years pass, and Adrian is leaving for college soon. I find him in his room scraping stickers off his door with a paint scraper. There's a puddle-shaped scar below his elbow from a fall that should've gotten stitches. A suitcase filled with socks lies open in the middle of the floor. "You planning on packing anything else?" I say.

"Eventually," he says.

"I've been meaning to ask, whatever became of Neil?"

"He got expelled. And then San Antonio and then juvenile detention."

"I mean what he's doing now."

"I have no idea."

"It's just strange. You were so close." My voice is sheepish. I sit on his bed. "Do you think you'll ever see him again?"

"Please don't sit," he says.

I leave his room and walk through the kitchen and out to the driveway. The ramp's Masonite has softened in the rain and dried in the sun, hollowed out to a light, inconsequential material. I lift it right off the nails, intact, exposing the slurred grain of the wood beneath it, and break it into pieces and stuff them into the garbage can.

A few months later I'm walking the dog through the park when I see a car docked haphazardly at the dumpster, someone removing boxes from the trunk. I call Neil's name and he looks up and his expression of self-possession disappears and his face goes mute and tolerant. His shirt is tucked into his pants and his hair cut short and gelled into ridges and there are tiny white buttons at the tips of his collar. I think his new respectability is touching. He was close to becoming someone else and chose against it. People generally accede to whatever will have them.

He tells me his father moved to the town houses near the club. He's living with his sister and working two jobs, and he names the places, warehouses. I should see all the product that's returned! Every object for any reason. Sometimes he's there all night but he doesn't mind.

The sky in early, early morning. It's like a mirror.

A Neighboring State

1.

When the daughter ran away, the mother and the father, who had allowed her much latitude, began to wonder, every second, what she was doing. For the father, this was a terrible question. His mind traveled to alleys, unfinished basements, bathroom stalls. He imagined that the daughter would be tempted not by money but by notoriety and something warm, like a cup of hot chocolate. The mother thought of other things. She pictured the daughter window-shopping along a row of sun-struck storefronts. She thought of her head emerging from a turtleneck sweater, the staticky lift of her hair. Life might actually be better without them around. After all, the girl wasn't really a girl anymore. She was sixteen. Her teeth were bright white and her gums the color of good salmon. Her laugh grew louder the longer she held it, like a bird made more specific against a darkening sky.

The father created a Facebook page so that people who might've seen the daughter could contact them. The mother spent all of her time at her computer instead of out on the streets or calling police stations or homeless shelters or bus depots or, for comfort, friends.

Talking to her friends was unsettling. None of them were surprised by the daughter's disappearance. They were ruthlessly prescient; the daughter had undertaken the most predictable of journeys. Talking to the daughter's friends was no better. There were deep wells between the words *she* and *said* and *late* and *party*. What was the mother supposed to do? Throw herself into them?

2.

The father knew better than to try to touch the mother at night. He probably didn't want to do anything either. The mother wasn't past her prime, exactly. Past implied too great a distance. She and the daughter had sometimes stood in different rooms regarding themselves in different mirrors. They understood by the quality of silence that the other was doing so, too. It was uneasy, this surveillance, and when they emerged it was as if with the results of a test. The mother had written the test and the daughter'd had to take it. It was passed down, the act of scrutiny. They both knew it.

No, the father was keeping clear. He was busy. Sometimes he was busy being still, and sometimes he was busy moving. This morning, he was heading out the door with a stack of flyers under his arm. "Why don't you come with me," he said.

The mother was wearing a terrycloth robe and woolly slippers while her daughter shivered and stamped her feet on some street corner who-knew-where, while she engaged in unsupervised who-the-hell-knew-what. "Let me get dressed," the mother said.

The father had a staple gun and a roll of electrical tape. He didn't simply paper bulletin boards and telephone poles, he papered over other people's flyers as if they were of no consequence whatsoever. He papered over bus stop poetry and the toll-free number of a vasectomy clinic, an element of vandalism to the enterprise. The mother was impressed. She strode to the front door of a bakery called On the Rise and hung a flyer there. She wanted to stop people midstep, stop them as they crushed toward their cinnamon-swirl bread.

The mother went inside, the father trailing her. She ordered coffee and stood observing the cashier, who looked to be a few years older than the daughter. The cashier leaned against the counter, propping her pregnant belly on its lip. Her big eyes drowsed on her face. The mother showed her a flyer.

"She's very pretty," the cashier said.

"Have you seen her?"

"See her? Not at all. Don't think so."

What barbaric equivocating! She carried her coffee away and creamed and sugared it lavishly. The mother in her mothering of the daughter had failed. She had failed to give her an instinct for return. The daughter had not scattered crumbs, not left a trail. Her backpack and some clothing were gone, as was a toiletry bag of the mother's covered in a pattern of jungle leaves.

The father came to her side. "Are you all right?"

She shook her head.

"Do you want to go home?"

Again she shook her head and they drove on, the mother cradling her coffee between her thighs. The father drove in a kind of appalled silence. Not appalled at the mother but appalled at what they'd created, this situation where they were driving around town looking for their sixteen-year-old daughter. His emotions were most visible when he thought he was hiding them. The mother felt his silence as blame, a palpable fuzz of recrimination that lay over his features like moss over stone.

They went to the food co-op, the library, two vintage clothing stores, and a coffee shop where the daughter and her friends liked to order sweet, elaborate drinks. They slipped a flyer under the door of a bar where she went to hear floppy-haired boys play electric guitar in all-ages shows. The daughter pushed her way to the front, arrived at the tips of the boys' dirty shoes. On the flyer, she smiled the father's half smile. She wore a pair of the mother's earrings, and squinted into sunlight that had long disappeared.

3.

The mother began to experience time differently. Seconds swelled to contain days. The mother replaced the batteries in all of the clocks in the house. She called her cell phone from the home phone, and the home phone from her cell phone. The mailbox filled and emptied and filled. She set the kitchen timer and listened to it sing. At night, time softened into dreaming, but in the morning it woke with a new severity.

4.

It snowed for the first time that year. The snow looked like sugar in the long grass. That night, the mother decided to sleep in the daughter's bed. She arranged herself beneath the thin quilt but was too cold to fall asleep. Why had the daughter never asked for a heavier blanket? She'd asked for Free People sweaters and 7 For All Mankind jeans and design-your-own Vans and sparkly gray eyeliner, but she had no language to want the practical. The practical lay outside the gilded cave of longing. The mother went to the linen closet and pulled out a comforter. The father came to the daughter's room and got into bed, too. His head close to the mother's on the daughter's pillow, he told her he was afraid he would never see the daughter again. He said he kept having nightmares that they'd found her, and arranged for her to come home, and just as she arrived, he died. The mother imagined that, and imagined that for just a second her grief over the father would be undone by seeing the daughter again, like an ugly coat unzipped to reveal a beautiful dress. She gripped the father's hands, the quiver of his fingers. She kissed his mouth. He returned her kisses and soon they were having sex in the daughter's bed. Change the sheets, change the sheets, the mother kept thinking. As if he could hear her, the father said yes.

5.

A message, an address. It came from someone who described himself as the daughter's guardian. He said the address was temporary. It was out of state. The father went to the police while the mother drove about town assembling things for a care package. She would send the daughter a package just as if she were away at boarding school. Boarding school was a place the daughter would've taken to. She'd always thought of herself in grander terms than the circumstances of her life made able. In the package, the mother placed lip balm, licorice, woolen boot socks, and, a splurge, a cashmere hoodie. *Hoodie*— the daughter hated that term. *Then don't wear it*, the mother argued with her silently. She added gloves, Little Hotties toe warmers, extra-strength Tylenol. The care package was becoming less fun. *Come home*, she wrote. *We miss you. You're forgiven.* But the daughter might not feel she needed forgiving. The mother could just see her pretty hands destroying the mother's missive. She tried again. *We'll settle down together, I promise. We'll find our peace.* But that felt too sanctimonious. *When you get home, let's pop popcorn and watch a movie. Your pick.* This sentiment was not really indicative of the mother's personality, and the daughter would see right through it. She placed all three notes into the box to represent her quandary. The father got home from the police station. He said the police were useless and he would go himself. There was still time. The state was a neighboring state. He could drive there in an hour. The mother made a sandwich for him. She gave him the package. "Call me as soon as you get there," she said, and they kissed as if he were going off to war. She watched the snub end of the car disappear down the street. If he did find the daughter, he'd never remember to give her the package, which was the best possible scenario except for finding the daughter *and* giving her the package, which was so unlikely it was what she hoped for.

6.

The father wanted to beat the shit out of whoever was with the daughter. Afterward, he'd feel beaten too. Then he could rise again.

7.

The mother loved calendars. The daughter loved big spans of open time. The mother loved warm weather. The daughter loved the cold. The mother loved reading, the daughter watching movies. The mother loved fires, the daughter loved the thud of water thrown onto smoldering embers. The mother loved eating. The daughter loved a small, precise dinner of virtually nothing. The mother loved the way the daughter looked first thing in the morning, before she disappeared into the bathroom to get ready for school. There were so many choices to be made when you were beginning to be beautiful, when everything depended on it. The mother also loved seeing how the daughter was attired when she emerged, how her hair was done. The daughter probably loved that less, because it wasn't the mother she was arranging herself for. It was the opposite of the mother. It was whatever was away.

8.

The father called to say he was at the temporary address. "And he's here," he said, "the guardian. He's got this sort of serf's beard."

"Surf?" the mother asked, picturing crashing waves.

"Like a worker on an estate. Like who Tolstoy tried to free."

"Oh. Is she there?"

"No," the father said. "He said he'd give her the package, though."

"Let me talk to him."

There was a scraping sound, and a voice said, "Yeah?"

The mother felt her right to her daughter rising empathically inside her, rushing upward like boiling milk. "Where is she," she demanded.

"Listen, she's free to go. I've got stuff to do," the guardian said.

"*You* contacted *us*."

"I'm trying to give her a nudge, frankly. A reason to leave."

"You fucker!" the mother said, but now it was the father on the other end.

"At least we know she's okay. That's the important thing."

"Ask him what she looks like," the mother said.

"I already have. He was exact."

"He saw her picture. Ask him to describe her voice."

"*I* couldn't describe her voice," the father said.

When she got off the phone she sat still to think. It was like . . . the daughter's voice was like . . .

9.

The mother flipped through a home decor magazine, and very quickly ordered puddle-length ivory-colored curtains for the living room. She would transform the house while the daughter was away, prepare for her return. Magnetic knife strips, double-stuffed duvets, actual made beds, cloth napkins. Knotty bars of handmade soap and scoured sinks and a small bowl of cured olives set out before meals. Signifiers of strength and contentment. The phone rang and the mother, thinking it would be the father, answered it. It was one of her friends, insisting that they go out to dinner. They sat with two others at a small table. Phrases slipped past her. *Cookie exchange. Closet organizer.* It struck the mother how laborious and wheel-spinning conversation was. One of her friends couldn't find her phone and another called it. It rang in some strange pocket of her coat, some subsidiary slit. Polite, polite, everyone was so polite. Finally, the mother found herself telling her friends about the message, the address, the trip the father was on, reliving it all when she wanted only the purity and possibility of solitude where what wasn't said didn't grate and rattle, heave and disturb. She had hope, but it was so hard to represent. She knew the daughter would return. But when she said *that*, it sounded too cavalier, though her friends rushed to agree with her.

"Of course she will," one of them said.

"She's getting something out of her system," said another.

"Something that she needs to get out, though it's hard on you," a third, who had a BA in psychology, observed.

"It's aimed right at you, actually," said the first.

The mother described how she'd ordered curtains that afternoon just for something to do, and everyone said that sounded like a great distraction, though completely perverse under the circumstances, she could tell they were thinking. Their words spun a trap that caught hers in it. She placed her words in their trap; she thought it was her duty.

She drank her wine. Her friends did too. "I've always admired your relationship with your daughter," one of them said. "Maybe it's the only-child thing, but you two seem as if you're equals, somehow."

"Equals," the mother said.

"What a great concept," said another, smiling.

They insisted on paying for her. As they walked her to her car, they passed a place where they could get martinis. "Let's get martinis!" they shrieked. It was much warmer and busier in this second restaurant, and the patrons were better looking. Old-fashioned light bulbs hung from long black cords above the tables and the bar. One of her friends removed her cardigan to show off her sleeveless black top arrayed with ruffles, her skinny, rugged arms. "The entire time we're here, will any men look at us?" she asked.

"Let's find out," another said.

They were there for an hour. Some men looked at them. Who knew what it meant.

10.

Late that night the father called to report that the guardian had gotten into a car and driven away. He'd watched him.

"So go in," the mother said.

"I have to get my nerve up."

"Where are you?"

"Just down the block."

"Stay on the phone with me," the mother said.

There was silence while he walked. It followed him down the cold, dark street, carefully, cautiously. The silence was its own small being, and the mother loved it. Tug on a word, tug out its thread, and this was what was left.

"I'm there," the father said, and she jumped a little. "I'm going to knock on the door." There were three sharp raps, and after a minute he said, "Nothing."

"Try the knob," the mother said. "Maybe it's open."

"I don't—" he started, and there was a creak. He whispered, "I'll call you back."

The mother went into the living room and sat on the couch. What was he seeing? She imagined the gray, heavy-bottomed scuttle of a rat. She imagined a wooden spoon with a glop of gruel stuck to it, a copy of *The Anarchist Cookbook*, an open laptop affixed with a bicycle sticker. Somehow the humble bicycle had become a daring and countercultural object.

It was snowing again. The mother used to suspect that the daughter was not a virgin, but now she was filled with certainty that she was, and this thought bothered her more than the former. There was something inevitable in front of the daughter, eager for completion . . . it made her want to hurry up, speed up like the movements of jerk-legged actors in old movies. She lay back and eventually she slept, and woke to the sound of a closing door.

A man with a stiff, cone-shaped beard stood in front of her. The beard looked as singularly poised for scrubbing as a toilet brush.

"Are you the guardian?" the mother asked.

"She says I am," he said. "She thinks I can explain her to you. She thinks because I'm not her I can explain her, fifteen and so alone."

"Sixteen," the mother said.

He had a flat waist and thin hips. The mother thought of him poised over the daughter, the snakeskin shiver of his biceps.

"She's scared of you. She said you want so much from others, you're greedy for their perfection. I said give your mom a break, you know?"

The mother rose from the couch and walked into the kitchen. She removed a bread knife from the large wooden block and when she turned around she was brandishing it. "Get out of my house," she said.

He smiled shyly and stepped closer as if to catch her by her elbows and hold her. She stabbed once or twice at his chest. Fluff puffed out of his down vest.

"You cut me!" he said.

Headlights roved across the window and she dropped the knife into the sink and went outside. Two figures got out of the car. It seemed to take them an immensely long time to approach. In the halo of porch light the daughter was smaller than the mother remembered, coatless, her boots pulled over bare legs.

The guardian pushed past her. "Don't go," the daughter cried.

The mother ran forward to stop him. If she wanted him she should have him. But he disappeared into the snow and when the mother turned around the father and the daughter had gone inside and the house was lit up like a ship on a white sea, moving carelessly, irrevocably away from her.

Love Not

She inquired brightly if she couldn't convince them to join her in ordering the vegan queso. When they hesitated she asked the waiter his opinion of it, and he said he always added chorizo to his. The nonvegan queso prevailed. Nate watched her from his side of the table. She was so unlike his mother, a linguistics professor who encouraged—no, demanded, but with a touch so unwavering he scarcely noticed it—excellence in both of her children. His older sister was now in her second year at Brown, and he, a high school junior, did many things—debate, saxophone, water polo—very well. You let your toenails grow when you played water polo, the better to stab your opponents in the depths.

She turned her animated face upon him and asked what his favorite class was, and he answered in a way that he knew would please her. He said AP English.

"Is that so?" his mother said.

She smiled. "I think it's wonderful. What's the last book you loved?"

He rattled off a title that his intellectually ambitious friend Xander lugged around in his backpack and quoted from whenever he could: *Ice Trilogy*, Vladimir Sorokin. He could picture the novel's cover, a lithe, alien's figure with a radiant head and dissipating white dots for skin, his profile down-tilted, pensive. One of the lines Xander was fond of was, "Oy, your balls are so hard!" Xander referred to their classmates as meat machines, and while Nate liked this description very much he didn't feel he had the right to use it. He would've had to have read the book, a not-insubstantial book, before he could do so but right now he felt free to lie in order to impress his mother's friend.

She said she'd started it and given up because it made her feel crazy, and she didn't like feeling crazy unless it was by choice. The nonvegan queso arrived. He ate steadily as she praised his part in trying to keep literature alive all the while literature was curling up and dying, how even in her house (and I work in publishing!) books were losing the battle to online news and cooking shows, an impotent lament he'd heard from others but was rendered more emphatic from her—her disappointment had a tactile, agitated quality, and it was as if she were growing larger and brighter and more wobbly right there at the table.

"That reminds me!" she said, and passed her phone—a respectably but not futilely old model—around the table so they could see a photo she'd taken. It was of a page of a religious tract she'd picked up in a Chinese restaurant where she'd gone for takeout. *The Television Set: The World in Your Home*, it read at the top, and below that, *Love not the world, neither the things that are in the world* (I John 2:15). *Among the world's amusements, television is a great villain on the highway of time.* "A villain on the highway of time," she repeated. She seemed enchanted by the phrase. "I'd argue the highway's the same but the villain's changed, multiplied. That's the thing about social media, its infinitude. Your finite life, the internet's infinitude—oh, it seems to me you *could* form a religion against it. Your generation, Nate, needs to do something—it's manufacturing your thoughts, mediating your experiences. The worst is that it's stolen the power of creation from you. Listen to me, I sound like an old lady."

"No, you don't," he said.

"I offer this as proof. The passcode for my phone? I got tricky with it—instead of 1234 it's 2345."

"Really? That's mine, too."

"Nate, it is?" his mother said. "That's ludicrous. You need to change that."

"I know," he said.

They were in downtown LA at a Mexican restaurant. Two girls sat at the next table, speaking in low voices and laughing and though he didn't allow himself to look at them he was aware of how their beauty kept him from looking, how its shine and the candles on their table made a little grotto of them, something to be worshipped. His mother's friend, on the other hand, was like a window display. Her curly brown hair rose in a dust cloud around her face, the long stems of her wind chime earrings scraped and clacked, and she wore a cracked green leather bomber over a T-shirt that hugged her breasts. They left the restaurant and walked to the theater where they were to see a musical she'd suggested. His mother had confessed to him on the drive in that she did not consider this musical real theater and was insulted that her friend thought it was the kind of thing she'd go for, though it was possible she'd had Nate in mind when she suggested it. Anyway, she *had* gone for it (out of politeness), and so had proved her friend, who would remain ignorant of her true taste, right, until she, in turn, suggested a show, though she didn't want to do such a hard pivot aesthetically as to embarrass her friend. It was nice not to be the object of his mother's concern, so in her pauses he kept saying *no, yeah*, agile phrase that worked in response to nearly anything. He sensed she knew he was placating her. Now he let them walk ahead of him, witnessing how their sides bumped, how they laughed and clutched each other's arms as if to steady themselves against laughter's unbalancing. The street was lit with strings of bulbs that crisscrossed low across the center, across the old trolley tracks. The plaza in front of the theater was crowded with people in dark coats. A man sang a song, its tune lilting and brave, with an upended beanie at his feet, and Nate's mother gave him a dollar to give to the man. He stifled the impulse to tell her that he was not a child who would thrill to the adventure of placing a bill in a man's hat anymore, because saying so would be taken by her to be far more aggressive than he would mean, and wouldn't be worth the ensuing conversation.

In the carpeted lobby, he found a restroom and changed his phone's code to 2345.

Their seats were arranged with his mother's friend in the middle. The show began. He moved his leg so that his knee touched hers. His mother coughed. It meant nothing. His mother's friend's leg was still as a log. He was just about to remove his when he felt her pressing back. It was like becoming aware of a numbness wearing off.

In the darkness of her bag on the floor at her feet, the screen of her phone turned bright.

At intermission, she stood and checked her message and put her phone back in her bag. "I may as well take advantage."

"I'll come with you," his mother said.

She left the bag on the floor. He slipped her phone into his pocket, and placed his phone where hers had been. They drove home in separate cars.

The next morning, he composed a text from her to his mother telling her that she'd enjoyed their outing. *Nate seems very mature. I can imagine doing many mature things with him.*

He was trying to amuse himself. He deleted it.

Fun to spend the evening with Nate! I don't know how it——teenager-rearing, oh the horror!——is done, but I know when it's done well!

Too many exclamation points? He thought of her fleshy belly and tapped the send arrow.

Next he texted his own phone. *Guess who?*

Shucks, thanks.

It was from his mother, a swifter reply than he'd expected and for that reason vaguely dismaying. He didn't want to think that his mother could take on this tone of false modesty, this quick coyness that meant she was human and greedy for praise. But she could, of course, and had.

He did homework and then went for a run with her friend's phone in a belt pouch meant for water bottles. Near the high school, on a street of ranch houses, he stopped, bent over, rested his hands on his knees. The yard he crouched in front of was landscaped with white gravel and gray-blue agaves. The largest of the agaves sprouted a thick central stalk like a giant asparagus from its skirt of spear-tipped leaves. The stalk rose four or five feet into the air, at least. It would blossom and then die. He'd seen entire agaves pulled onto their sides by the weight of the toppled stalk.

A man emerged from the house, shielded his eyes from the sun, squinted his way. Nate sprinted away, slowing to a walk as soon as he was out of the man's sight.

In the bathroom after showering, his mother's friend's phone buzzed. He punched in her code. There were four texts from someone named Ian.

Looking forward to seeing u in Frankfurt

Like to alert u to a new technology bound to bring u great satisfaction

No guesses?

Calling it my print on demand penis

Another buzz, this time from his number.

I know who it is. No mystery there.

He sat on the side of the tub, legs weak.

Haha, he wrote. He was ashamed of himself.

Trying to work. Your phone's blowing up.

Sorry.

Someone named Natalie seems convinced if she texts every 10 secs you'll eventually text back.

Good old Natalie: slip-on Vans and high-waisted jeans, little daubs of fuzz over her upper lip. She was president of CALF (Care About Living Freely), the animal rights club. He was president of STEAK (Students Toward Eating All Kinds), and there was social pressure for them to date because they were on opposite sides of the issue and it would be cute plus a real fuck-you to the disgusting adults who couldn't conduct themselves civilly anymore.

She's usually right, he replied.

Meet me at Seebing's and we can talk about your little sleight of hand.

He rode his skateboard there in flip-flops, tucked his board under his arm, and went into the grocery store. She was standing near the deli counter, regarding a small bag of gumdrops she'd plucked from a table that held bags of different kinds of candy tied with ribbon. He backed around the corner, followed her down the aisles. She wandered aimlessly, at one point drawing his phone out of the back pocket of her cutoffs to check the time on it. Her elbows were red. A blue vein rose from one of her calves, abruptly changed direction, subsided back into her. A woman he recognized—another of his mother's friends—greeted her and he could tell by her guardedness that she was desperate for the woman to be gone, that she was only going through the motions of conversation, engaging in an empty back-and-forth, and this pleased him. To know she was thinking of him, distracted by him. Finally their voices raised and thinned to the notes of leave-taking. She headed toward the coolers where he met her. "I'll be outside," he said.

She joined him a few minutes later at a white plastic table, sliding a root beer to him.

"Thanks," he said, taking a sip.

"Check out those toenails!" She uncurled his hand from the can and spread his fingers and slipped hers into the long notches between them. "These nails could use a trimming, too."

"I might be in love with you," he said.

She let go of his hand.

"But I'll act like I barely know you when I see you."

"You do barely know me," she said.

"Feeling like this is a kind of knowing." He was proud of this insight, proud that for the first time he'd expressed himself exactly as he wanted to express himself. This was the beginning, he thought. He had been so stupid and thwarted but now everything was changing.

"Whatever it is you're feeling," she said gently, "is predicated on not knowing me."

He blushed. "Can't you just accept a compliment?"

"Here's the thing, and sorry, I'm lecturing, but that's not a compliment. It's about you."

He was considering his reply, something along the lines of she'd better take compliments while she could still get them, when she spoke again. "But I will say I recognize that you're going through something. I used to fall in love so easily. I fell in love with someone because of the way he stood up from a chair. It was like his knees unhooked themselves from his body and he floated upward and was ours for the taking, the people in the room, and I had better claim him before anyone else did. I'd've never noticed him had he stayed seated."

She was wearing sticky orange lipstick and her teeth, misaligned, made a clicking sound like sifting ashes. He thought he might throw up she was so appealing.

"*I* would've noticed you," he said stubbornly.

She smiled and he felt tears slosh behind his eyes, press against their dark chambers.

"Nate, you're going to be absolutely great. You are great. You feel deeply if erroneously." She patted his knee. "But I need my phone now."

He slipped his hand in his pocket. "Shit," he said.

"You don't have it?" She paused. "Did you forget it?"

"Sorry."

"That is inconvenient. Can you have your mom bring it by my house?"

"What would I say?"

"Tell her it fell out of my bag at the theater."

He stood and knocked over the soda and brown fizz ran down his leg. "That musical? It was lame," he said.

At the end of the block, a car slowed next to him and a voice called, "Do a kickflip!"

It was Fisher, from water polo. Mindlessly he took a push, took another, barely got off the ground and slapped back down gracelessly.

"Weak."

"Look at my shoes."

"You should be able to do that shit barefoot. Where're you going?"

"Nowhere. My mom's friend left something at our house and I'm getting it for her."

"She hot?" Fisher asked.

Nate's chest tightened and began to drum, and he laughed to cover it up. "No."

"Sure?"

"She's like late forties or something."

"So? Erotic knowledge, son. Think how appreciative she'd be."

"I doubt that," he said.

"I'm just playing with you," Fisher said. "I'm a virgin, to be honest."

They all were. The radio towers on the foothills looked like toothpicks topped with cellophane frills. At home, the kitchen smelled of coffee. There was a dusting of grounds on the counter with a circle in the middle where the Chemex must've stood, and on a cutting board a knife and a rind of cheese and the diffuse red blots left by strawberry tops. The domesticity irritated him. The little human pieces. Upstairs, her phone was next to his bed. His thumb stroked back and forth, back and forth over her smeary screen. He could peel the blue rubber case off, he could imagine her drawing one arm and then another out of her bomber jacket, one leg and then another out of her jean shorts, but all he actually had was this.

He went into her photos. A man showed up again and again. Dark bangs fell over his forehead like a crow's wing. He sat at a table littered with wine bottles and she bent over him from behind, her arms draped over his shoulders, her smile bewildered by pleasure. He couldn't believe the man would sit like that, turned away from her. He deleted every single one of him, and then others, the religious tract, a grocery list, ash trees against a violent peach sunset. Then he dropped her phone in the trash, knotted the bag, and took it out to the bin in the driveway. He'd tell his mother he lost his— she'd grumble and make him retrace his steps at school and the pool, and then, for her sake, she'd buy him another.

But she didn't succumb so easily, and he was phoneless for nearly a month. Finally, she drove him to the Verizon store.

In the car on the way home she said, "Jill—you know Jill—seems to think you're depressed. She said she saw you downtown the other night, and you were silent, glum."

"Who uses the word *glum* anymore?"

"She does, obviously. She said it looked like Natalie was trying to cheer you up but you wouldn't go along."

He remembered the occasion. They split a pizza and then walked around, holding hands for a minute. He was feeling a horrific laziness about being animated, amorous, seventeen. "How does she know who Natalie is?"

"I pointed her out to her. She was curious," she said.

"Great, so you guys have been stalking me."

"Hardly stalking when it's your mother."

"Not you. Her."

"She cares about you. She's taken an interest." His mother paused. "You know she doesn't have kids of her own."

"I can see why not."

"Nate! You're being rude."

"I don't mean to be," he said. "And I don't think there's anything insulting about saying that. Actually, I think it's a compliment."

"Certainly she has a tolerance for being alone. An ability to be who she is. But not having a family was a disappointment to her—in fact, she wanted it more than I did."

"Dude."

"Don't sound so shocked. When I found out I was happy, of course."

"Both times?"

"Both times."

"Well, phew. Does Brenna know this?"

He'd long suspected that his sister knew more about his mother than he did.

"It's not a scandal, Nate. Nothing to know, per se. Anyway, are you? Depressed?"

"No."

"Sure?"

"Yes."

They pulled into the driveway, where he was confronted by the plastic garbage bin. "Thanks again," he said.

In his room, he flung the bag on the bed and sank into his bean-bag chair. He was on the verge of beginning something with Natalie though he felt her attention as invasive, not welcome. Still, he needed her now more than ever. He needed to turn to her and kiss her openly on the mouth. He needed to live his life as though she were always watching. *She*, not Natalie. Natalie would come and go, one of many kind strangers who would pass through. That wasn't too bleak, he didn't think. Maybe he was wrong. He should hope he was. But as he sank lower and lower into the mush of the chair he felt

a profound, pancaking thud inside him and heard a voice instruct-
ing him to stay like this in acquiescence, that this was where he'd
find her, in this pause, this posture, this conducting silence, this
tunnel through which he might crawl to her and enfold her in his
arms. To die for love seemed suddenly the most sensible thing in
the world. Yet at the same time another, stricter voice told him to
sit up straight, unwrap the phone, activate it and call her and tell
her that his love for her *was* about him, and that was why it couldn't
be vanquished or set aside or talked into submission. She was right.
It made him who he was, and would carry him into other rooms
and other times and other people's lives, like a haunted conquering
alien whose gentleness they saw and mistook for human.

The Artist's Wife

I had high hopes for being friends with an artist, but as it turned out the artist's wife found me hopelessly uncool—a seething boredom came over her face whenever we got together—and the artist's art was much too expensive for me and my husband to buy. I'd only ever seen his paintings on his website where they lost the intensity my husband claimed they possessed and seemed simply to blare. They depicted smooth, seal-skinned figures in scrubs laboring in operating theaters and over dentists' chairs. In one, the figure, legs planted far apart, tugged at the teeth of a bear trap. In another, the figure removed a porcelain doggie holding a little red heart on a loop in its mouth from the cavity of a child's chest. In a third, I wasn't sure. A grotesque surprise awaited one, I supposed.

The artist was always high when he worked, my husband said. He would get too bored otherwise.

I blamed myself for the situation with the artist's wife. I'd worn jeans and a flannel button-up to her birthday party at a restored bowling alley in Silver Lake. The bowling alley had gleaming wooden floors and orange sherbet–colored molded plastic chairs. The wife was wearing jeans too, with patent leather high heels, and I supposed that made all the difference. She was a teacher at a Waldorf school, and many of the guests at the party were parents of children in her 3/4 class. The men were bearded and broad, with thick, soft shoulders and mighty calves that burst out of their fanciful socks. The women were cautious, assessing, their eyes oracular and their faces so sharp-boned they appeared antique.

When we arrived, neither the artist nor his wife introduced us to anyone. This would be fine if we were in a living room or a backyard where you could attach and remove, attach and remove, and there were always a few people in the kitchen eating chips, but the alley was cliquish, the guests clustered in small groups laughing over their gawky ministepping on the lanes and high-fiving when someone bowled a strike. I got separated from my husband (rather, he separated himself from me), and ended up bowling a silent game with another solitary guest. We simply found ourselves at the same lane. My bowling ball was much too light and skittered across the slick wood as if across a licked popsicle. His ball was heavy, thudding, and strangely effective.

He was attractive in a haggard way, and I considered that there was no female equivalent for that.

I'd worn the flannel and jeans because that was the kind of thing I wore. I knew I looked as if I were picking out paint samples at a hardware store or trundling recycling to the curb, but I didn't mind. Undertaking some common endeavor, in other words. Living in the world, as men did.

Snatches of conversation floated our way. "Finally I said why does *Cole* always have to be the monster?"

". . . plowed right through a migrating cloud of painted ladies. I couldn't freaking slow down!"

When the artist, my husband in tow, approached the silent bowler and they began to talk, I realized two things: one, I was the lowliest person there, for the artist had approached him, not me; and, two, the silent bowler and I had a lot in common but we hadn't let ourselves discover it.

We had in common our taste in music. We had in common a self-conscious laugh.

We had in common a certain stance toward the world. I gathered he was a fellow sufferer.

Cake was being served. I accepted a large piece and gobbled it up, then fled to the car.

I slipped my socked feet out of my bowling shoes, climbed into the back seat, and curled up on my side. I let my mind drift. I thought of my past, college, riding buses, tumbling golden leaves. (Leaves tumbled here in December, papered the sidewalks obligingly.) My second year of college, I rented an apartment with a girl I'd known since childhood. We thought it would be funny to read bedtime stories to each other. In my memory this plan was devised by both of us, but it was probably mine. She twisted and turned angrily in her bed as I read *The 500 Hats of Bartholomew Cubbins* and the first few chapters of *The Wolves of Willoughby Chase* and then she began staying out very late at night. She'd realized our plan smacked of the desperation of people who wanted to be cheered, and the fact that she had come to this realization before me—though surely I was on the cusp of it myself—meant that I was solely responsible for how she felt. She left notes taped above the kitchen sink that said *Do your fucking dishes* and *Take out your trash*. *My* trash? I thought. I let the phone ring when I suspected it was my boyfriend calling so he'd think I was out with friends. I'd listen to his cheerful voice leaving a message, a voice from a distant land.

I returned to the bowling alley and stood next to the long silver rack where the balls were kept. A strange idea came to me. We were in one of the artist's paintings, I thought, and in that painting his wife carried a whip like a black rat's tail and if she deemed you a poor guest, stilted or boring or awkward or frazzled or uncomely, the painting came to life: a trapdoor opened beneath your unlucky feet and you fell a short distance onto a heap of bodies. I could practically feel the sudden lurch, the swing in my gut as I plunged down onto a writhing pile. I apologized profusely as I rolled off to the side. We were in a storeroom. The silent bowler was there too, squatting on his heels. He did not look pensive though he should have looked pensive. We heard the clicking of the wife's high heels coming down the stairs, whip rasping behind her. An iron key rattled in the iron lock and the heavy door groaned open. She spoke to us sharply and assigned us impossible, mind-numbing tasks. I was given a toothbrush and told to scrub the mold from between the honeycombed stones of the walls and floor. The silent bowler was told to polish the tiny, high window using his own palm and saliva.

We were the painting's janitors, its silent labor. Every work of art was supported by people like us.

The wife left. Guests kept plummeting through the trapdoor onto the pile of us, and we rearranged ourselves bitterly. We did not ask each other how we knew the artist or his wife. One way or another, suffice it to say. From here or there, why would it matter? What mattered now was what had been taken away. To have one's shine dulled so completely, to be tumbled in with those whom you frankly *could* conceive of belonging here . . . well, it was dispiriting. Let's talk, someone said. Let's stay human to each other. Goat cheese, yay or nay? Improv, embarrassing or freeing? Do you follow any of the organized religions?

My husband strolled by the rack and I reached out and grasped his arm. "Where are you going?"

"The bar." I trailed him there. He ordered a beer and received a tall sloshing glass. "Want one?"

I shook my head. A slim arm tattooed with dark blue script reached between us to accept a drink. The artist's wife. I happened to know that the tattoo read *With pleasure* in Russian, a language she could not speak.

She clinked her glass against my husband's. "Can I get you something, Cathy?"

"Oh, no thanks. I had a corner piece of cake. I'm bursting." I looked at my husband. "I think we're taking off soon but this was great!"

"Not that soon," he said.

I was the assistant to someone who ran a lecture series at the college where my husband taught. I didn't get to choose who came. I arranged for travel and accommodations, made sure they got paid, picked them up and dropped them off at the airport. I was glad not to have to choose who came because if the readers were clumsy panderers or culturally illiterate or excessively sweaty, it wouldn't be my fault. At the last reading, the writer had gotten up in front of the audience with nothing in hand, no sheaf of papers, no book. She stood at the podium and said that just that afternoon she'd decided to abandon the novel she'd been writing, the novel she'd been planning to read from. The problem was her distance to it, she said. She'd never figured out her distance to it. And she'd realized something else: it wasn't about life. And there was *ab-so-fuckin'-lootely* nothing she could do about that. The director of the lecture series cast a desperate glance at me, so I went to the front of the auditorium. Any questions? I said. Later she told me it would've been better to thank everyone for coming and point them to the coffee and refreshments in the next room. Because what questions could anyone possibly have after that? the director said. Does she think that one book is about life and another isn't? Does she think life's so recognizable? I regarded her with interest and she went on. Our first stories were populated with gods and monsters, she said. Take *The Odyssey*. Would someone say, well, that's not about life because there's no such thing as a cyclops? Because Polyphemus doesn't really exist? No, we understand human ingenuity, the longing to go home. And we understand too that it's never easy, that all manner of monsters might spring in our way. Must spring in our way! For if it were easy—to go home—we wouldn't want to. So for her to stand up there and offer no explanation to our students, who, after all, are not well versed in failure, who have, possibly, *never failed in their lives* . . . it left a bad taste in my mouth.

Maybe it wasn't the monsters that were the problem, I said. Maybe it was the longing that was missing. The director cocked her head and seemed to entertain the idea for a moment. But longing's the easiest thing in the world to invent, she said. Throw some longing in the pot! Stir it up with an absent father and a moldering trunk of old letters! My god, writers act like it's so hard. They should talk to surgeons or janitors or home health care workers or me. Or you! she said, startlingly, because I'd never thought she thought much of my job. The next morning, I drove the writer to the airport. I was tempted to tell her how easy what she had not done was. I scrutinized her for sorrow and humiliation but observed only a tendency to shield her mouth with her hand when she talked. She spoke to me, behind her hand, of her love for her Instant Pot. When I pulled up to the unloading zone, she removed her hand and bid me good-bye as if we were old friends, throwing her arms around my neck and pulling me close. I'll read whatever you write whenever you write it, I said foolishly. Thank you, she said. You don't know how much that means to me, but I'm going to massage school.

The artist's wife and my husband had ordered a second round of drinks. "His gallerist gets half of what he makes," she was saying, "and he likes her well enough but how much do you have to like a person to be okay with that?"

"A whole hell of a lot. You have to want to pay their mortgage on their summer house in the Hudson Valley," my husband said.

"Or, in her case, Venice."

"Venice!"

"It's outrageous," she said. "With all its sinking."

"Why can't we just get over Italy?"

"About his paintings," I said. "Do you understand them?"

She blushed and I softened toward her then. The bloodlust of the other discarded guests would be rising. They would've figured out they had to work together to break the lock with their combined strength, wrench open the heavy door, scale the stairs. They were about to pour back into the alley, and whose side would I be on?

"I'm thirty-six," she said finally. "I'm done trying to understand."

A woman who knew she was younger than the woman she was talking to would always mention her age if she could.

"It was his idea to have my party here. He thought it would be easier than having it at our house. Less personal. Safer."

My husband was nodding. "Let me show you something," she said.

"Me?" he said.

"Colleen."

I followed her to the end of the lanes as if we were after an errant pin, through a door, and down a flight of stairs to the storage room. Gold paint peeled off the door knob. A waxing and buffing machine stood in the corner next to a mound of orphaned bowling shoes. A small canvas leaned against the wall. She picked it up and hugged it to herself. "My birthday present. It's a portrait. Other men take their wives to dinner," she said, and turned it to face me. The paint was thick and the woman's forehead hideously bulbous not in the manner of a holy figure of thought but rather someone about to burst with consternation. Her bun sat atop her head like a tiny, shiny gourd, and her eyes were splayed unevenly, as if to avoid catching sight of each other, yet there was beauty in her face. She would not see it. She would not see how he saw her. Love, if it meant anything, was private, lonely, inexplicable. "Do you like it?" she said.

My husband and I left and drove east to the town where we lived where the bowling alleys were not restored but were big, cold, raucous places. To know that the artist could paint like that, create something so true it became continuous, not a fixed image but an experience of looking, made his choice to paint anything else incomprehensible to me, cruel. I did not think it was safety he was after but its opposite. I exited the freeway. At the end of the off-ramp a man stood next to a plastic bucket of roses in chemical colors. He had other things for sale too. Fuzzy blankets folded over a line. Lidded cups of fruit. I lay awake that night trembling with eagerness for morning.

Blades in Silver Water

The summer before Emily went to college, she worked as a babysitter for a night nurse with an eleven-year-old daughter. She arrived by bus in the evening to the girl eating toast and marmalade while the mother drank a cup of coffee. "Let me show you where you'll sleep," the mother said. She led her upstairs to a small room whose bed was made with a pink comforter with felt buttons and told Emily she would return at six-thirty the next morning, but that she should feel free to keep sleeping and leave whenever she woke up on her own.

"The comforter on that bed used to be mine," the girl, whose name was Stephanie, said when the mother had gone. Her pale-yellow hair fell down her back and she wore a T-shirt that read *Christmas Tree Lighting 1983*. She went to the window and folded her hands on the lip of the sink and watched her mother back out of the driveway. "I grew out of it."

Emily carried her plate and the mother's cup to the sink. She'd had a pita bread with a slice of Swiss cheese and one lettuce leaf at four o'clock. She dumped a clot of marmalade down the drain. "It looks soft," she said. She put the plate in the dishwasher and rinsed the cup in the sink and followed Stephanie out a sliding glass door that led to a concrete patio surrounded by pink and purple azalea bushes.

"Winberg!" the girl called.

"Yeah," a boy's voice replied.

"What are you doing?"

"Same as you."

"No you're not. I'm with my sitter and you're alone."

Emily went back inside. The town house had a drugstore smell and wall-to-wall taupe carpeting. The brick- and vinyl-sided house where she lived with her parents and younger sister was unkempt: sandals and dog leashes and brown apple cores and dollhouse furniture and *Washington Posts* scattered everywhere. She longed to live in elegance and simplicity, but first she had to go to college and then she had to break up with her boyfriend. When she lay in her boyfriend's bed listening to the burbling of his fish tank and watching the shining tetras nudge their sunken treasure she felt a kind of recognition that scared her. She would break up with him as soon as she wasn't lonely anymore, she would keep him around until that moment.

Her mother did not want her to take the babysitting job. She didn't think it was safe for Emily to stay in a strange place overnight. She was a worrier when Emily wanted a friend. Was that unfair, to ask from her mother a little levity and cheer? She knew her mother could not give it to her and still she asked for it.

In the kitchen, she found a container of Maxwell House French Vanilla Café instant coffee, examined the calories and fat content, and scooped the powdered mix into the mother's cup. She filled it with boiling water from the instant-hot knob and carried it out back. Stephanie was doing a handstand, her long legs splaying open and shut to keep her balance. She wheeled into a cartwheel and stood up. Her face was flushed. "What are you doing now?" she said.

Emily imagined saying trying to make a kingdom out of shit, thanks very much.

"Meditating," Winberg said.

"On what?"

"It's private."

"I won't tell anyone."

"It's you I don't want to know."

Stephanie turned to Emily and rolled her eyes. "Are you going to be able to sleep tonight do you think? I'm up all *night*. I have insomnia and I asked my mom to bring me something but she won't. She could. She could bring something home *so easily*. She's a bitch."

"You shouldn't say that," Emily said.

That night after Stephanie went to bed she lay on the couch reading. She became aware of a sound, a mechanical growl. She checked to see if it was the refrigerator, then went out back and stood on tiptoe and looked over the fence into Winberg's patio. A beach towel printed with lemons was spread over the concrete. The air conditioner rattled. Back inside, she wrote a note to Stephanie and left it on the TV doily. The sound was louder in the parking lot. She locked the door behind her and threaded through cars, passing a walled-off area of trash bins. Light was coming from the Springfield Mall, from the multiplex.

There was a landfill not far from here. Maybe trucks opening their bellies to the dump were the source of the noise. A pigeon pecked at a nub of pretzel in a parking spot. Headlights slid over the pavement and the oil-spill sheen of the pigeon's neck and the fat front tire of a car rolled right over the bird. She waved her arms too late. "Didn't you see him?" she cried.

A man got out and slammed the door. The bloody toupee lay at his feet.

How quickly things went from one way to another. She returned to the town house, got into bed still dressed, and curled on her side.

At some point she became aware of a figure in the room. "Stephanie," she said in a whisper.

"Yeah."

"What are you doing?"

"I told you."

"Told me what?"

The girl didn't answer.

Emily sat up. "Told me what?"

"You're not human. Don't come back tomorrow."

"I have to."

"I'm going to tell my mom not to let you." She flicked the overhead light on and off.

When Emily was a child she would wake in the night and call to her mother for a glass of orange juice. Her mother would bring her the juice and the taste of it, the mystery of its being there so cold and sweet and suddenly at her lips tasting of another time, of the morning when everything was possible, made the deepness of night clear to her. "Stephanie, you know she's deaf to you. Go to sleep," she said. The girl left the room.

In the morning the mother said Winberg's mom had collected Stephanie and taken her and Winberg to the pool. She offered Emily a fruit cocktail from the fridge.

"You should've seen what I saw last night. A man came in with his feet clenched like fists. Balled up completely, his nails cutting into his soles. He said sometimes he got leg cramps but never this before. He could only stump across the floor," the mother said. "He was in agony."

Emily ate a pineapple bit. "What did you do?"

"Gave him a muscle relaxant and watched those things uncurl."

She asked her what the doctors she worked with were like. The mother answered that they were tyrants but she didn't mind because they treated her well, they were very respectful. It was telling however that patients sent *her* the thank-you cards. She had a connection to them. She had seen them at their lowest point when they were actually quite adorable.

"Stephanie came into my room. She said she has a hard time sleeping."

"She says she has a hard time with a lot of things. Well, I guess she does. She's not imagining it but I'll tell you what, she makes it worse." The mother yawned. "See you tonight."

As Emily rode home she considered that she didn't have to return. She had a choice. She wasn't trapped. She could get a normal job at a coffee shop, or as a page at the library. She'd like that, pushing the wooden cart forward, stopping and sliding books back onto shelves. She'd like that they had a certain place, that there was a system. The alphabet, how much it made clear.

She walked straight upstairs to her room and lay down and sleep came like a bag over her head.

She woke to a knocking. "Scott called," her mother said.

Emily called him back standing at the end of a long coiling phone cord stretched taut into her room. He said they should go to Virginia Beach, that he knew a place to get meatball subs. She took a shower and returned to the town house. When she lay on the couch to read, the growling began again. She stiffened and became absolutely attentive. She couldn't help it. Her ears tuned themselves to the frequency of what she listened for and then she felt herself, like a clockwork figurine, jerked forward by the sound.

She got up and went into the kitchen. Stephanie was upending a bottle of chocolate syrup over a glass of milk.

"I hate my stomach," the girl said. The plastic bottle wheezed and gasped and her spoon clanged merrily against the glass.

"That's inane."

"What's inane?"

"Pointless. Stop stirring for a second."

"I know what it means. What's inane about it?"

"It's like hating your heel or your shoulder or an ottoman or something. Listen. Do you hear that?"

"Hear what?"

"Hear *what*? I don't believe it."

"You sound like my gym teacher Mr. Snelson. He's always saying we should speak within ourselves and leave him alone. But all we wanna know is how to do a layup!"

She went with Scott to Virginia Beach. A man had drowned before they arrived but the beach was not closed. Sometimes they closed a body of water for a drowning, a bystander told them. They sidled up to the water's fringe and let it splash their shins. Death lay shivered over its surface. Scott had his caricature drawn. Tiny teeth, long chin. He gave the sketch to Emily and immediately she conceived of where she might stow it before she disposed of it. She would not like it beneath her bed like a broken mirror. Perhaps shoved far back on a closet shelf. They took the train to New York and stayed in his cousin's apartment. His cousin was a flight attendant. They had sex in her bed and went to a Horn & Hardart Automat and let their coins fall into the slot, opened a glass window and removed a slice of chocolate cream pie and ate it in alternating bites. The train home rattled like a toy in a pneumatic tube.

The next evening, she returned to the town house. The girl wanted desperately to purchase a back-to-school black purse with fringe, the mother said. She had given her the money.

They set out on foot. The man from before was unlocking his car. "Remember me?" he said.

"Hello," she said, "and no."

"The pigeon? Careless of me."

She shook her head but she knew he could tell she was lying. "Who's your friend?" he said.

"I'm babysitting her."

"Babysitting. That's neat."

"She's been at it all summer and she's not very good at it," Stephanie said.

He laughed. "I bet you're all right. Want to get in? Your friend can get in the back."

"No thanks. We're going to the mall."

"I can take you," he said. "My name's Samuel."

"No thank you."

"*Please* let's," Stephanie said.

"I like her insistence," he said.

Instead of driving them to the mall he drove to McDonald's and offered to buy them milkshakes. She didn't recognize where he went after that. No Pizza Hut or Sizzler looked familiar though she had eaten in those establishments on other streets like these with power lines like wet hair caught in a comb's teeth and black gas station gallon numbers against a white board like a theater marquee advertising the cost of living. Stained glass lamps dangled on gold chains over booths, the waitress brought breadsticks. If you returned to that booth often enough you'd never leave it, not really. Something humble and greedy and diminutive would lodge itself in you. They passed a self-storage facility, rows of corrugated metal buildings with closed padlocked doors. One door stood open to a jigsaw-jumble of furniture. The growling was enormous here. It was light out but the light had darkness behind it like glue laid over the back of a sheet of paper.

"You're beautiful girls," he said.

Stephanie's straw scraped and guzzled at the bottom of her cup.

"I used to be a scout, a talent scout, so I would know. I'd walk the streets looking for that it factor," he said. "I'd go to malls, hair salons, grand openings. Dog shows. You wouldn't think so but a lot of beauties go to dog shows. I'd sign the girl, I'd set her up with everything she needed. The mother, though, that was interesting.

The mothers of beauties are a whole other category. The genes took a turn somewhere. It's interesting to see, human genetics. The family tree. I spot a little seashell, perfectly scalloped face, long hair, gleaming eyes. A girl named, say, Gail. She'll be renamed but she doesn't know it. These are Gail's last moments, sitting at a table drinking a Coke, legs crossed at the ankles. A young girl crosses her legs at the ankles, an older girl higher up. So, I look over the table to where the mother's sitting. I can barely see her, there's something blocking my vision. It's like a shadow moves in, a floater. But the girl *loves* the mother."

"That's funny, because I hate mine," Stephanie said.

Emily twisted around and slapped her face, then pulled back, frightened.

"Darn it, why'd you do that?" he said.

They were on a residential street lined with single-story brick houses and trees with heat-limp leaves, at the end of which was a soccer field. Two figures dangled off a goalpost. Beyond that, a broad unmarked expanse of grass flooded by the creek that ran next to it. Blades in silver water. Emily unrolled her window to the humid air.

"Please take us to the mall," she said.

"You act like you're nothing, and that's dangerous. You have to act like you have someone waiting for you, someone who knows you're gone."

"I know she's gone," Stephanie said quietly.

He turned into the parking lot. The department stores were closed and she got out and stood in the desolate patchwork of spaces. Stephanie was still in the car. "Let's start over. You're okay. You're going to be okay, right," he said, and the girl clamored like a wounded animal into the front seat. The asphalt was cracked here, where she was standing. It began to rain flat heavy drops. But why do you ask. We are undefended, she thought.

Old Poets

He tried to weigh his soul to see if it was a poet's soul.
—James Joyce, "A Little Cloud"

The day before my husband and I were to leave for the conference I succumbed to the horror of packing, standing and staring into the closet at my limp, unassuming clothes. My phone buzzed with a text from a friend who was en route that day: *The worst place to fly out of to this thing: Boston. The airport is crawling w 62 year old poets who were horsewhipped by Robert Lowell at BU 40 years ago and have spent the time between then and now in a damp cellar, among the root vegetables, writing sestinas about their wounds and working on their accents.*

My husband texted back, *One of the many benefits of flying out of Ontario, CA: there will be very few literary types on the flight with us. Maybe some crusty, desert rat acolyte of Gary Soto. I don't know what's more tragic, young poets or old poets.*

To which I responded, *We're all of us old poets.* Meaning we were all tarnished brass. I was depressed. The novel I had written was not going to be published. I had longed for sensitive readers, intuitive readers, readers who might upon arriving at the final page think *You know how when you sweep spilled sugar off a tabletop into your hand*

& feel all the individual crinkling little grains? It was like that **OR** *I don't know how we got here but I like where we ended up* **OR EVEN** *What the hell?* Instead they said, some with kindness and others curtness and one agent with a kind of proximal horror, No thanks. The book was a failure, or I was, and now I had to go to a conference full of people who were not failures, or who had wrapped their failure in bright paper and made it pretty, adept in the art of subterfuge and reinvention as I was not, and walk among them and make small talk, and see old friends, and act as if life went on, which, undeniably, fortunately, it did.

The next day, we flew from Ontario with indeed only one other literary type on the plane (horn-rimmed glasses, *My Brilliant Friend* spread across her lap while she gazed at her phone) to the city where the conference of Writers, Editors, Educators, Poets & Students (WEEPS) was taking place. In the car on the way to our hotel, we passed makeshift tents pitched on the steep hillsides that lined the highway, precarious arrangements of tarps and blankets fitted onto what must've been the faintest exhalation of flat ground. The driver asked my husband if he'd ever heard of Shakespeare. My husband said he had. The driver said Shakespeare's themes were surprisingly modern, the way he wrote about paranoia and obsession and jealousy. My husband agreed. Yeah, Shakespeare was cool but he didn't really read anymore, the driver said.

"What do you do instead?" my husband asked.

"Smoke cigarettes."

At the hotel, we were given a tiny room with a stuffed pineapple on the bed. I was not a larger-than-life person, not an up-all-night person. Sometimes it seemed that all I did, what my whole existence came down to, was buying bags of hamburger buns at the grocery store, examining the plastic tabs stamped with sell-by dates, riffling through them to find the freshest. How dire my patience was!

We went to a Vietnamese restaurant for lunch. I gulped down

my banh mi and scurried outside to a parking lot to take a call with
the last agent on my long, long list who'd expressed any interest in
me. I had assumed that because she'd suggested we speak by phone
she was going to say that she wanted to represent me. Actually, the
agent wanted to talk at length about what kinds of manuscripts
she'd love to fall in love with and how one of her writers had a habit
of popping into Indian restaurants to take a pinch of those candy-
coated anise seeds they kept in little dishes on the hostess stands.
They sounded more dismissive, I was sure, than she meant it to. As
her conversation moved further and further away from me, I, too,
became abstract to myself, a gawking onlooker, an eavesdropper, my
ambitions ridiculous. Finally I interrupted her to say I had to go,
I had a panel to attend. (I had no such thing.) My legs were weak.
I had imagined telling an interviewer that I wasn't going to say my
novel was like a baby because what male novelist would say that,
though it was too bad the simile was suspect because it was actually
pretty accurate: the novel had kept me up at night, it had been help-
less, it had seemed somehow less peachy and fuzzy and pleasantly
shaped than others I had seen but I had loved it for what was in it,
what was *me* (cue fear that I'd never really allowed it to become au-
tonomous, itself). But it didn't matter now. My husband came out of
the restaurant and looked up and down the sidewalk and when his
gaze landed on me his expression gripped my heart, squeezed until
I felt its jellied exterior give way. I shook my head. I had given myself X years (+ or -) to write and teach only sporadically and now I
would have to get a real job. I lay on my stomach in bed and perused
the classifieds on my laptop while he showered. Jobs these days required fluency in computer programs I'd never heard of, the helm-
ing of social media platforms, tons of experience. It seemed no one
could do anything for the first time anymore, you had to have already done everything for *years* and be willing to report to a desk at
eight in the morning and remain there until five o'clock. Impossible,

I thought. It would take me hours to get ready in the morning. Shaving my legs alone would spur a crisis of indeterminate length. I shaved in the summer but not in the winter and it was late spring now. I'd look at the classifieds again when I'd started shaving.

That night, we met the friend who'd texted us at a brewery filled with noise and laughter and rough-hewn tables with long uneven benches. We went around the table listing the most memorable name of any student we'd ever taught: Virgil Hightower, Olivia John Newton, Cry Freedom. (On my roll the girl had been Madeleine Brown.) We talked of the ignominy of publishing. "This is the worst business in the world," our friend pronounced cheerfully, and I felt my spirits lift.

The next day, my old college boyfriend, who lived in the city where WEEPS was being held, picked me up in a car that smelled of wet wool and took me to brunch (pungently yolky eggs with peppery greens and hunks of molasses cornbread). Afterward, we walked in a park among rosebushes that were not yet in bloom. The bushes were skeletal, precise, frozen in their postures of waiting, and I was struck by this and felt it announced something about the conditions that gave way to beauty. You bloomed only after your pauper's heart was laid bare. My ex-boyfriend said he was still trying to figure out what he wanted to be when he grew up, and I knew he said this because he thought I was trying to figure out the same and I wondered what had happened to have stranded us like this in middle age, what calamity of passivity. Had we stayed together we'd be the proprietors of a bakery, probably, rising early in the morning and working contentedly side by side for we had liked each other's company, that was what our relationship had been based on, a safe, easy kinship. We would've had two or three little children with clown-splotched, food-stained mouths, and he would've toiled happily for them, making sure they ate well and played outside and got good and dirty, leaving me to be a distracted mother. He possessed an utter innerness, a complete quietude that was seductive. I wondered what would happen if I told him to take me to his place so we could fuck. We traversed the park and the adjacent neighborhood, and he showed me a house he'd nearly bought with his partner, a frankly freckled woman I'd met once whose breasts had seemed to sit rather low. I didn't want to notice that her breasts sat low but I had noticed, and so all I could do was neutralize the judgment behind the noticing. I admired her bralessness, I decided. My ex-boyfriend said the house was part of a communal living arrangement and they were relieved they hadn't gone for it because one of the residents was in a polka band, another was a woodworker, and a third was a yoga instructor.

"What would be wrong with that?" I asked.

"She'd be humming with self-righteousness," he said. We returned to his car and he drove me back to the convention center.

Inside, I ran into my husband at the entrance to the book fair. He'd eaten a gummy and thought the crimson carpeting was obscene and was absenting himself immediately. I bid him goodbye and wandered through the cavernous room, passing tables displaying the bright faces of literary journals and books from small presses, until I came to a table advertising a low-residency creative writing program whose gatherings took place in a variety of European cities: Barcelona, Amsterdam, Berlin. No one was there. I sat behind the table in an empty chair. It felt nice to perch somewhere for a moment. A pair of young women walked past. "Stories full of Milos," one of them said.

"Fuck Milo, fakest name ever," the other replied.

I slung my coat over the back of the chair. An acquaintance from grad school days, a woman I saw once every few years at this event, came to a halt in front of the table. For the past ten years she had been writing a biography of Joan Aiken, and the longer it took her to finish the book the more worthy it seemed. A thin gold thread ran through the fabric of her scarf like a root's endeavoring tendril. We hugged and exclaimed over the unsurprising surprise of running into each other.

She plucked a glossy brochure from its stack on the table. "Nice gig if you can get it!"

"It really is," I said.

"I'm still at _____ but I'm fishing. I'm always fishing, I guess. Do they stagger faculty here?"

Writing was an act of invention, but the practitioner of that act was supposed to hew precisely to facts? "Thankfully it's a regular thing," I said, and transformed myself in that instant into somebody who had something that at least one other person wanted.

A modest gain, I realized. But I felt a sly kind of stamina take hold of me.

"I'm looking for something regular," she said. She had crinkly hennaed hair and a wobbly orange circle of unblended foundation on her temple. "It's so exhausting not to have something regular. Might you put a word in?"

"Of course," I said. "And maybe"—I tilted my head as if struck anew—"you could connect me to someone about reading at _____?"

"Oh, absolutely!"

Her face turned grim the second she walked away. Neither of us would do any such thing but that didn't matter, what one was after here was the transaction, the getting-oneself-out-there, this gentle prostitution, this mortification, this delight.

I glanced at the headlines on my phone. A *New York Times* article titled "How to Travel without Leaving a Trace" I read as "How to Travel in Place." I checked my author's website and found it had been taken over by a website that sold Dickies. A young man in a brown cardigan approached the table. He fretted over its buttons as he addressed me. He was a poet who felt dicey about writing about himself because as a cis white male he was pretty sure his voice didn't urgently need to be heard right now. "Well," I said, "I think your sensibility informs whatever you write, whether it's about your own experiences or not." The young man looked relieved to have found a way for it to be okay to sort of write about himself. After he'd gone, I thought about what I'd said and decided I was wrong. Probably you should fight to keep yourself out of your writing as much as possible, in any way you could. Probably that was what had gone wrong with my novel—I had polluted it with my peculiar way of seeing the world, my jagged little leaps of faith. I had built an unsteady edifice, its walls made of paper, and I had lit it on fire and then asked others to enter it, to enter the little pyre of my dreams.

We had dinner that night with two sets of friends at a restaurant on the top floor of a hotel. To enter the restaurant you walked through a short dim tunnel lined with neon tubing, like the entrance to an aquarium. The food was very expensive, and I felt guilty that our friends had to spend so much money to eat in this restaurant my husband had chosen by googling best restaurants in _____. We didn't have that kind of money either, and the choice of this restaurant, I thought, presented an erroneous picture of our taste and predilections to these friends we hadn't seen in some time. The table was extremely wide and long and it was impossible to talk to anyone but the person right next to you. Luckily, I was seated next to the only other woman there, a tall, beautiful creature I'd known for twenty years. We spoke of Jonathan Franzen's girlfriend's essay about envy, how it was too bad that that was what she was known for when she was a fiction writer herself. We spoke of wall-mounted heated lube dispensers. Sometimes I wonder about us, the woman said. The accommodations of our desires. The waiter kept bringing dishes to the table—sweet potato and apple sushi, broccoli with fat cloves of garlic, steamed buns filled with peach and tempeh—and we'd take modest helpings and the dishes would disappear to the vastness of the table. We spoke of a mutual friend who was in Guatemala on a Guggenheim. Some among our ranks were still achieving. We heard bits and snatches of other people's conversations, Lucia Berlin, Jake Phelps from *Thrasher*, provosts. We did not think to have the waiter take a photograph of our group. It wasn't that we didn't feel nostalgic for each other, it was that the table had flung us too far apart.

I walked with my husband under one of the bridges that straddled the rivers of the city. It was a beautiful day in a place frequently beset by rain. We moved through a teary cloud of urine. Someone offered us chicken curry. When we came out onto the bank and stood looking at the big brown buildings and smokestacks on the other side of a river the gray of grime-coated glass, I considered that the post-industrial was even more melancholy than the frankly industrial and was glad we lived where we did, where the sun was hot and heavy during the day and the air sharp and cool at night. The temperature rose and fell like a set of old-fashioned scales. Yellow blossoms bleated from bushes, purple petals frothed from jacaranda trees then dropped to carpet sidewalks and grass, little purple trumpets that attracted bees. Someone squeezed my shoulder and I turned to see an editor who had passed on my novel. I knew his wife, and asked after her. "She's at Nordstrom," he said. Do not let humiliation capsize you, I thought firmly. His wife was at Nordstrom. I had written a novel that would not be published. And yet, to look at us, no one would think we suffered, or would think we suffered more than we did. How little anyone knew of anyone else! How we lorded ourselves over some and debased ourselves to others when in likelihood we'd gotten it the wrong way. I lapsed into silence as we walked, allowing my husband and the editor to pull ahead. All was hype and misunderstanding and occasional glimpses of the trueness of shapes, a profile, a shore, an animal, a tree. Our friend who'd been with the young woman at the brewery leaned against a railing at the entrance of the convention center, but I couldn't appreciate him as I would have the other night because I had seen him for the first time already, yet seeing him then had been undercut by his company. I strained for a moment of illumination, that graceful moment when a person appears familiar and unfamiliar all at once and years arch and collapse like a deck of shuffled cards, but it was just him, canny and slight and smiling crookedly, and I introduced him to the editor and we all went inside together.

We wandered around for a while, laughing. We were old, but we weren't the oldest people there. Our particular demographic would know what you meant if you wondered why Dean Wareham had left Galaxie 500 just when everything seemed to be going so well. To be free of the responsibilities of home, to be aimless and irreverent . . . we probably all had the same books on our shelves and records stacked next to our turntables, we were virtually interchangeable, you could put us in a dark room and we'd know whether the Levi's we were unbuttoning were 501s or 512s, our desires predictable, our transgressions so legible to ourselves we were already writing the scenes in our heads. We passed the European writing program table and I saw it was unstaffed again, so I told them I was off to get a coffee and doubled back and sat down. Clumps of people drifted past and pulled apart, occasional singular pilgrims finding their way to the shrine of the table. I talked easily and readily to them, I opened myself up, I had nothing to lose. When the day had grown late, I wrote my email address on the last few brochures stragglers took.

We flew home. In my inbox, an email from the registrar at the college where I occasionally taught, whose subject read "The seven kinds of bowel movements" and another email sent a minute later that read, "Toothaker, Linda would like to recall the message 'The seven kinds of bowel movements.'"

There was also an email from an address I didn't recognize. *It was so great to talk to you at WEEPS about _____. I really like your attitude! I'd love to work with you but you're not listed as faculty. Are you new? Best, Carla.*

Carla, Carla, I thought, but could summon no face, nor could I recall what attitude I'd taken. Self-mocking, I supposed, my go-to posture. *They're prehistorically slow in updating their materials*, I replied. *I'd love to work with you, too. Are you new to writing?*

I threw in a load of laundry and returned to my computer, where there was a response waiting. *Writing's been a lifelong passion of mine but I've never had time for it until now. I quit my job, actually I was fired for kicking a hole in a wall (it was an accident!!), and so I decided this was my chance to really devote myself . . .* I read on, lulled by Carla's industry and earnestness, Carla from Camden whose novel was set in Prohibition-era Brooklyn and was populated entirely by dogs.

The only real story is the passage of time, I wrote back. It was the truest thing I could think to say.

Thanks, that helps a bunch, Carla replied.

I emptied the kitchen cabinets and scrubbed them with vinegar and hot water and soap and lined them with contact paper. I rearranged the furniture in the bedroom and bought a new mattress to put on the old frame, and new pillows and a new comforter. The shower curtain was plastic, and I threw it away and bought an organic cotton curtain with a tasseled hem. My taste exceeded my means. Or not taste exactly but a feeling made material, given shelter in a shower curtain. Where was the money going to come from to pay for this? The royalty checks my husband and I received each year paid for approximately one extra-large pizza, and some years no pizza at all. Still we ordered what we referred to as our phantom pizza. Carla emailed saying she was struggling with how much detail to include in a sex scene she was writing, and I replied that a sex scene was warranted only if the reader learned something about the characters at the end of it that they didn't know at the beginning. *Well, Mavis, a Dalmatian, has been courted by Miles, a Boxer, for a long time,* Carla responded, *but they've never been alone together before. So you'll learn alot.*

I tossed and turned on the new mattress. My husband, a deep sleeper, was unaware of my restlessness. I had stopped talking about my novel, so he had too. How quickly the defeats of others grew muffled and abstract, like the snow on the mountains we could see from our house. The snow fell without our feeling it, yet still it fell. It landed, resolute, beautiful from a distance. Fixes and revisions, necessary changes, narrative-cohering movements occurred to me in the night with startling clarity, and I jotted them down in a little notebook I kept bedside. But in the morning, when I opened my laptop and stared at the screen, those fixes quickly became impossible, the foggy remains of a dream.

What was that Muriel Rukeyser quote, that if even one woman told the truth about her life the world would split open?

Did I *want* the world to split open?

On the one hand, the world—it was obvious—was overdue for a reckoning.

On the other hand, what if the numbers stayed low? *One* woman? What if no one else joined in?

I was afraid of being alone in my honesty but I didn't mind being alone in my cowardice. No one would notice me then.

Carla emailed to say she was struggling to write convincing dialogue that didn't sound fake, and I composed a reply quoting

Edith Wharton, *All that was understood between two characters should be left out of their*—but no, enough of that. Enough wisdom. Instead I wrote that I was sure it was going to be terrific, something so crisp about the word *terrific* and encouragement, I'd realized, was all anyone really wanted.

My office looked out over the backyard. It had been a rainy winter and everything was blooming, yellow yarrow and ice plants, crimson bougainvillea, red-tipped ocotillo. Even the cactus had sprouted a small protrusion that meant another slow arm was coming.

A friend who was getting divorced was consulting a healer, an enlightened being who told her things about herself that other people couldn't know. The enlightened being traveled all over the world and now she was staying in a hotel in our town, and my friend invited me to meet her. We drove to the hotel, and on our way there I relayed to my friend something that was bothering me. Recently my mother, who did not normally tell stories about our family, had told me over the phone that when I was a baby and we were driving from the town where my father had gotten his PhD to the town where he was going to do a postdoc, he had warned my mother that if there was an accident she would have to save me because he intended to save his dissertation, printed out and bound and in a box in the trunk.

"That's wild," my friend said.

She parked in a spot reserved for hotel guests. The enlightened being was sitting in the courtyard beside a fire pit filled with bits of blue glass. The enlightened being said hello. The enlightened being said we looked beautiful in our clothes. The enlightened being asked if we agreed with Kant's assertion that morality was not the doctrine of how we make ourselves happy but how we make ourselves worthy of happiness, and we said that sounded about right. The enlightened being looked relieved. Most people are greedy nits, she said. We ordered water. The enlightened being removed the sliver of lemon speared on the side of her glass with her teeth and tossed her head to fling it into the fire pit. She had been to Dubai, Mykonos, Aspen, Santa Fe. She toted around a tiny tent—custom-made—that she pitched at the end of her bed under her covers so the covers would not touch her feet, and she spoke of the challenge of taking this tent with her everywhere she went and pitching it over and over again in new places. She did not say why she preferred the covers not to touch her feet, which in their leather sandals were long and serene. She spoke only of herself and I assumed that the comments my friend had thought referred particularly to her were in fact statements plucked from the morass of experience at the enlightened being's disposal—in other words, that the adhesive quality of pain led you to think, when words gave it shape, that it was about you, explained you, scooped out your marrow, etc.

There was an email from Carla waiting for me when I got home. She had been admitted to the European low-residency writing program, and was looking forward to seeing me in Barcelona, it said. *Congratulations!!!!* I wrote, then deleted one exclamation mark. *I was thinking all along why the hell are your characters dogs, but it seems that someone, at least, didn't agree with me.* Carla took a few days to reply and when she did she wrote that not only had she been admitted, she'd received a scholarship and had specifically requested to work with me but the director had no idea who I was. It was sad, she wrote, that I'd felt the need to lie about teaching in the program, but maybe now *she* was in a position to help *me*, maybe she could put in a good word for me. She knew what it was to try to elevate yourself a little because you've realized that if you don't, no one else is going to. If you don't toot your own horn, who will? She had lied in the past for just that reason. To be a word in someone's head. She'd always suspected that people didn't respect her and if I felt the same way—if I just wanted *some respect*—then she understood, she really did. But what she'd learned was that lying wouldn't make them respect you—in fact, they'd respect you less. Anyway, good luck and all that.

I closed the email and hesitated, then brought the curser over a folder with some story scraps in it, things I'd been meaning to go back to. It wasn't respect I was after. Of course it was existence.

Origin Story

Alabama

Hotel room where they waited for a garage to order a new clutch for his Honda. The clutch had gone out not even halfway through their cross-country trip to Arizona, where she lived and where he was moving. One spaghetti-stained issue of *Harper's* between them, football on TV. She escaped the room to walk through the plant nursery behind the hotel, mounds of funereal dirt beneath black plastic sheeting. Savage cold. The sound of oncoming traffic was her life so far, and the sound of it receding was her life now. Cupping her hands to peer into the greenhouses, saplings like blind white worms. She'd always romanticized the wrong turn, the unknown road, the forsaken place, but now that she'd found it she realized it was the imagining she'd loved. The sky was colorless, like a surface someone had worked to scrub out. Waffle House, syrup shining from its pitchers. Running across the highway to the garage. The creatureliness in her limbs, the car sitting there like a trussed animal. Photographs of dead deer thumbtacked to the wall, the mechanics raising cigarettes to silent faces. She was foreign to them, and, to be fair, they to her. Someone had not loved them once, and so they got very close to things, like suitors in camouflage, and delivered the shuddering final shot and bent over the body and touched it. They might've liked to touch her, too, wade with their hands down to her heart. It felt like that in the garage. That the men it contained contained themselves a violence that lay in wait for exactly her youth and impatience. She returned to the hotel. To the part of her that would live in that room forever, is there to this day. Finally they were told the car was done, and he went to get it while she packed their things. They hooked the U-Haul to it and started off. As they accelerated up the on-ramp, the clutch broke again.

Arizona

Vine-scrolled back house. The bathroom was doorless, a tolerable inconvenience for two people newly in love. She hung from the doorframe a pink batik sheet patterned with elephants walking trunk to tail. They called out to each other as they showered. She biked their sheets to the laundromat, zigzagging around broken glass, watched the sheets tumble, biked home again. The thing was, the fucking thing was beauty was all that mattered and she would never have enough of it. The world would hold it in reserve because she wanted it too much. She saw beauty in nature, in the mountains piercing the sky through the jellied light, but as for herself saw only a smudge, a crinkly edge. They drove south to Bisbee and hiked up the mountain to the shrine at the top, a series of hollowed-out rocks whitewashed and painted with blue-and-green birds, beaks pointed to earth, feathers clutched to their bodies like soft plummeting pine cones. The hollows were filled with votive candles, crosses, pictures of dead children, tinsel, plastic flowers, cherub statues, pinwheels. She assumed the children were dead. It would be wrong, would it not, if they were alive, to leave them there.

Wisconsin

Second-story apartment in a three-story house. They moved to Madison because they had a friend there. The friend wasn't a close friend—he had the potential to be one, but they didn't know him all that well. When they arrived they found that his life was already full, that they would be his thirtieth friend while he would be their first. He had a wife who made pie crust from scratch, an office in his house with glass-fronted bookcases and a crystal decanter of whiskey on a silver tray. The friend was playing the role of writer more thoroughly than she'd imagined possible. It made her jealous and filled her with contempt. She thought writing came from seeing, and seeing came from never being seen yourself. She remembered everyone she'd ever met. The scabs at the corners of second-grade Veronica's mouth. The bright red iodine on her knees. She could go on, remembering. It was easy. It asked nothing of you but your stillness. For you to light a candle and see where its smoke went. One night, at a bar with bewitching tea lights on the tables, it seemed they had arrived, that the words could come pouring out of their mouths, that they could claim and wonder and parry and rise the next morning and drink a clear glass of water and get to work. But they fought. She felt for the car keys in her pocket and wavered upward from the table. Lights everywhere like a field of low-blown stars. But she went the wrong way, toward the bathrooms instead of the door, and had to turn around and walk by him again. He reached out and stopped her, and they were instantly reconciled.

Florida

Old carriage house. They were teaching at a community college, but she had a breakdown and left midsemester. She found work as a theater usher, read *Paris Review* interviews on a silk sofa in the ladies' room lounge while latecomers inched down the aisles unaccompanied. She was no Charon, no dark-river guide. She was a gatherer of the small things one needed in life. She drove to the mall to buy pillows. He stayed home and took a nap. While he was sleeping, a man broke a window of the carriage house, smoked a cigarette on the couch, climbed the stairs, and entered the bedroom. He woke up. The man ran. She was driving home listening to *Tigermilk* on the tape player. It was winter. Is it more accurate to describe winter in Florida, or Florida in winter? One occupies and the other, radiantly strange, is occupied. The moon was a frozen pond, its surface scratched by the claws of birds. She went to work at the seven o'clock performance. One of his friends came over. They built a fire in the outdoor fireplace and smashed beer bottles into its mouth and watched the glass melt. Suddenly flames came leaping out, licking up the wooden sides of the house, sparks drifting, lifting, rising with the ragged motion of mosquitoes to the roof while in the theater snow fell, a glittering mass that the stagehands would sweep into mounds with long brown-bristled brooms to use again. It was the Christmas musical. She heard the bells and singing through the walls.

Washington, DC

Basement apartment of a row house. The owner was never at home. He gave them a key to the upstairs and it was a good thing he did, for one day there appeared a ballooning in their kitchen ceiling, an udder of plaster leaking water. They positioned a bucket beneath it, ran upstairs, and discovered that the source of the leak was his freezer, a cave of melting permafrost with one white piece of wedding cake inside. His refrigerator had come unplugged. They called him and told him what was happening, and while he summoned a plumber they wandered around his living room, looking at diplomas in silver frames, Yale, UPenn, a class ring suspended in a glass cube.

Years before, she'd mailed her high school boyfriend's class ring back to him in a padded envelope. Browned masking tape wound around the band to make it fit. They had been conventional together. They had eaten popcorn shrimp together. He had moved his mouth over her carefully, like a metal detector over a field. The plumber arrived. Not long after that, the row house was sold to a newly married couple, young but older than they were, already successful, prosperous. The woman had a baby. The baby's cries came through the roof. One night the baby cried for a long time, piteous and raging and thin, and she knew they weren't answering the cries deliberately, that that was what they thought they had to do.

Ohio

Split-level in Yellow Springs. Her grandmother had died unexpectedly, and they moved into her house where they could live rent-free for a year. There was a grapefruit still in a bowl on the dining room table. She watched as it grew smaller and smaller and its pink blush dimmed, as it turned from an object of the ordinary world into a symbol, and she realized this was how religion worked, to eternalize not humans but the things they had touched, the places they had been, to make sure there was reverence and permanence in a world so porous you might fall through its cracks at any moment. Eventually, she tossed the grapefruit into the trash. They got married in a courthouse in Xenia with matching platinum rings they bought at Rita Caz. She wore a thrift store dress of red-and-white zigzags, he a pale-green leisure suit with a sharp collar. Her hair was cut very short. The judge asked if they were in the military. Afterward, they ate soup for dinner, and while he built a fire she went into the backyard with the canvas sling to get more wood. She felt so happy picking the pieces off the stack. A staggering abundance laid out for her like this.

Iowa

Plum-shingled cottage with a baby in it. Snow on the sidewalks, snow on the steps, snow in diamond treads in the entryway briefly before melting. Lollipop-colored light from the stained-glass window. She read *In Cold Blood* next to the baby with a book light shaped like a glass page—you laid it over the page you were reading and the words glowed with a sort of docility. The hushed room, the baby's breathing. She had to fight to stay awake and sometimes she lost the fight and a woolly haze enveloped her as if she were a plane passing through clouds. The morning after the tornado struck, they strapped the baby into the bike seat and took a tour of the damage, the sorority house whose roof and south wall had been sheared clean off, the rooms with their posters and pink bedspreads exposed. They stopped at a café, everyone being extra courteous to everyone else, handing out water, speaking cheerfully. They had escaped death, and though they knew it was blind luck they also felt a little special for it. Saved for *some* reason—for being nice, perhaps! Later, this café became the place she would go when she could get away. She'd order coffee and cake and stare at the screen of her laptop. Freedom wasn't to be found in words but in being alone, sitting by herself, thinking thoughts that would not appear in her stories because they were shameful in their intimacy and small in scope, the product of a lack of imagination or will or knowledge or something methodical that gave rise to what men wrote.

Pennsylvania

Bungalow beside a battlefield. Eighteen-wheelers wheezed past the house at five in the morning. Their son was friends with the son of the man who had hired him to teach at the college for the year. The man was the something-something at the college, and he was the something else. The boys attended the same preschool on the grounds of a shuttered Putt-Putt golf course. The children played in the abandoned windmills. The teacher wore the long skirts and flats of the indeterminately religious. There was a shag of tall grass at the field's edge, into which their cat disappeared. She wandered its periphery, calling for her. The second day of the cat's absence, she knocked at the door of a neighbor who was reputed to keep raccoon traps. The man wavered at the threshold, eyes beady as a bird's, not quite believing that she wanted to come in. She did. She wanted to see. Stacks of newspapers. A tilting, feral light. The traps were empty. She turned to leave. The man was drunk. He opened his arms as if to say all of this could be hers, his heavy body, its broken kingdom. Who hasn't been confronted with collapse and wanted just for a moment to catch what's falling? And then to stay low, stay lost? She returned to the field and commenced calling again and this time the cat trotted out on her small paws, meowing, curling, her teeth hungry and white.

California

Ranch in the Inland Empire, no Pacific Ocean, no beaches. He had a job on a campus of seventies-style buildings in the foothills of the San Bernardino Mountains. They bought a house thirty miles west. Freeways like the thick beige coils of firefighters' hoses. She wore a black velvet blazer to teach her class, pretending to know what she was saying. She knew enough to know she knew more than the others in the room, maybe. Or maybe not. That was the mystery of being alive. You walked around unprotected. The winter rains came. In the mountains the rain was snow. In the valleys the snow was rain. There was no country here, only landscape. And cars like enormous cattle, cattle reared on blood and suet, roving and fat and free.

Vermont

Vinyl-sided rental. Walking home after taking her son to school, parents biking past her, trailers empty of children, fleece blankets flapping over the sides like tablecloths pushed askew after a meal. Only one man said hello to her, a father who arrived on foot to collect his kid around the same time she did. He was younger than her but his son was the same age as her son. She invented a history for him, becoming a father in his early twenties, love and strife and separation, a minimalist kitchen, cologne bottle shaped like an art deco building. He was handsome, his hair close-clipped, his expression firm. She turned away. Sometimes it seemed as if they'd moved to Burlington for the sole purpose of eating muffins and cinnamon bread. Dark at 4:00 p.m. Their neighbor's house strung with white lights in plastic milk jugs. Finally the winter was over and the last day of school arrived. She passed the young father shooting baskets on the playground court and stopped to watch. He made a graceful, arcing shot that swept perfectly through the net, and she let out an ecstatic cry. She wanted to show him she felt something reckless, that having been pent up made her reckless because even now, in June, as a light rain fell, you were only a few months away from winter and all that secrecy and scuttling again.

California

White stucco box. Life resumed much as it had been before they left, though some people regarded their return with suspicion. They were teaching at a different college now. Small personal planes puttered at regular intervals over their heads. She gave a reading at the college and afterward a student said, "We were right there with you," and she realized that what she'd written was the desperate scrabbling of someone trying to tell a tale. But the tale would not be told that way! Finding the mints their son was using to mask the weed on his breath the day she slipped a ten from his wallet to tip the dispensary driver for her gummies. He wanted to be more awake. She wanted to be more asleep. A friend had a stroke, and she began going to her house to listen to her read from a simple children's book. Before they read they talked, and sometimes never got around to reading. One day her friend, with the use of a cane, went to the shelves near the fireplace and removed a thick black photo album that she opened to pictures of herself in a white bathing suit in Greece. Her friend was so young, but it was the quality of the *time* the photographs captured that made her cry. I don't know why I'm crying, she said to her friend. Later, she told him about it, how unashamedly she'd cried. They were walking along a path under a cluster of ash trees. They left the shade and moved into the sun and heard a crack and the shearing of something plummeting through brush, and turned back to see a branch lying across the path, jagged at the rip, the raw color of a newly sharpened pencil. They went to it and tried to lift it. As thick around as a marble torso, with that odd posture of a gesture interrupted. The flesh of the soul, she thought. They took a picture of it and texted it to their son.

Dogwood

To be in the world is to witness the birth of the constructed without seeing the death of the real. I remember when the world was real, and assume it was for some time after I last paid attention, not knowing everything was ending.

·❧·

When I was a girl, a woman who lived on my street scolded me for climbing a tree, telling me it was the Virginia state tree, that I shouldn't climb it. The tree grew from a strip of grass on the street side of the sidewalk. It was perfect for climbing, with a knobby, humped trunk and low branches, budding but not yet in bloom. Maybe the day was gray. Maybe the woman carried the memory of its powder-white blossoms inside her, the memory of the future I was threatening, less with my climbing than with my freedom to shape differently the vision of the tree the woman saw, a vision that should not bear the weight of anyone's body.

·❧·

Soon after I gave birth to my son, I felt pain that I ignored. I was used to ignoring pain, pain that folded itself into other pain and gradually dissipated, but this time it was sharp and singular. It began in my lower back and traveled down my left leg until all I could do was lie in bed with my husband's winter jacket tucked in the sway of my back. Finally, my mother, who was visiting, insisted I go to the emergency room. So I left my son with her and my husband drove me to the hospital, two weeks to the day after he drove me there to give birth. I don't remember what the nurse who first saw me looked like, I just remember her saying in a direct and unsurprised way, It's probably a blood clot.

Direct and unsurprised because what human finds misfortune surprising? Perhaps if you live among saints.

They ran me through with a dye that lit up my veins from the inside, that made my body feel warm and wet. They kept me there for two nights and gave me thigh-high compression stockings and needles to take home. I lay on the couch wearing the stockings with their rubber grips as my husband pinched my lower stomach into a petal of flesh and slid the needle in. The small child who lived across the street rang a ship's bell again and again.

When it was time for our son to learn to sleep alone I had to leave the house so I wouldn't hear his wailing, so I wouldn't race into his room and pluck him from the crib where he stood with arms raised.

He possessed a perfect knowledge that I'd save him and it was this I fled, this certainty about me. I pulled on my long thrift-store coat, and got into the freezing car and drove the streets of Iowa City past houses where I assumed all the children were sleeping peacefully, their faces like the surfaces of frozen puddles. You skated over their acquiescence. Their parents weren't bothering with the dishes, there was music on—their little tykes could sleep through anything!—and conversation and low laughter, not the moat-water silence of our house when our son was sleeping, the wood floors tiptoed carefully, the dog compliant in his bed, the phone's ringer turned off. I drove aimlessly, sobbing a little, and when I returned home I returned to a holy silence.

~

I was a zealot, as many new mothers are. Still, when my father called my son a tyrant, it stung. I was sensitive and my father was insensitive. All my life there's been this imbalance. Now my father is seventy-seven. The skin around his eyes is dark. His hair, which has always been black, has lately become shot through with white. Maybe not lately. Maybe it happened years ago and I'm only now noticing.

~

A small sheet of notepaper, mixed in with dry leaves at the end of the driveway. In looping black cursive it says, "*I miss the delusions of youth, my secret suspicion that what I felt to be the dimensions of my soul had never been so poignantly charted nor with such meticulous sensitivity and depth. My only ambition then was to turn this secret knowledge—this internal depth-charged map—inside out for the world to see. Imagine a flock of—*"

~

And I do. Something unclenches in my mind. The freedom, the logic of the wheeling.

~

The house where I live with my husband and son is small and slightly dirty, but every now and then a peacefulness descends from on high, and I don't know where it comes from or how to summon it again. How to call back the invisible? This is the endeavor of the religious and I am not religious. This is the endeavor of those who believe and I do believe, I believe in the stymied, the disconsolate, the failed, the forgotten. I believe in the ruined, the shamed, the awkward, the ugly. And then, out of nowhere, that peacefulness, which recasts all those figures in gold.

~

In the kitchen, I mistake a pair of crumpled boots for a cat dead now five years. Mottled black and gold, sitting with tail curled around her tiny paws looking out the sliding glass door and then gone. My realizations are like that too, a quick uncovering of truth before it returns to the impenetrable, life's realism.

~

A couple come over for drinks. They are smart and witty and I enjoy their company though it's hard to get a word in with them. I laugh, quip, sip my gin and tonic. But tonight something happens. I try to say something and am interrupted, and this time the man notices. He turns to face me. I can feel the weight of his gaze, radiant with patience, like a drop cloth draped over a plaster statue. My husband's talking but the man continues staring at me, stubbornly fixated on letting me say whatever I was going to say. There have been times when I've been drowned out midobservation and had to listen to someone else making the point I was going to make, eliciting the reaction I'd hope to elicit, getting the credit for it, crass though that may sound, and was annoyed, but this time, this time I had nothing to say, I was only offering filler, fluff, some banal and transitory sentence. My husband talks on, and I watch him as the man watches me. He watches me listening. This is how I'll be known.

❧

Among the voices, my silence unspools inside me like a thread of saliva blown back by wind.

❧

My class reads excerpts of Joe Brainard's *I Remember*. Joe Brainard throws his glasses off the Staten Island ferry in a fit of despair. He scratches his cheeks so people will ask him about his scratches and he can say a cat scratched him knowing they'll know a cat did not scratch him. I say here you can see how one memory exerts a mysterious tug on the next. I say this is an exercise in radical truth telling, and I ask the class to write some of their own I remembers, to write quickly, to not dwell. After a few minutes I say I'll get us started and then you should just blurt yours out, don't wait for me to call on you and don't worry about interrupting each other, you'll fall into a rhythm, you'll see. *I remember a freckled boy who played trombone in the high school marching band, how he aimed his trombone at the stands*, I read. *I remember doing push-ups until my arms trembled*, one of my students says. *I remember getting high with my cousin for the first time*, says a second. *I remember that airplanes smell like the vacuumed welcome mats of fast-food restaurants*, says a third.

⌁

The boy stood with torso tilted back, legs planted, the golden bell of the trombone raised. He was the passenger in a car that struck a tree on New Year's Eve of his senior year. The driver, a bass saxophonist, survived. He did not. I remember his wake, the open casket. I remember that his father, the funeral home director, had placed his trombone in the casket with him. The long body lay there unmoving. The morning of the last day of that school year, my boyfriend's car ran out of gas on our way to school. We drifted to the curb and got out and stood watching the passing traffic. A maroon Buick pulled up behind us, driven by the boy's father. He unrolled the window and offered us a ride. Any exams left? he asked after we'd climbed in. Just music theory and then we're done, my boyfriend said. That's good, the boy's father said. It's a mystery where music comes from. The thought of writing a song. He shook his head. Of course I've seen the power of music. The ugly brick buildings of the high school came into view.

⌁

Now I wonder how he kept himself from taking us to his place of business. Everly-Wheatley Funeral Home, meet these two who are not so different from mine, after all, so how is it that they stand here and he does not? How is it that the world is so irrational, so bereft of reason? Are not humans the architects of reason and buildings and the great stages upon which all of our dramas take shape?

I am the man who oversees their sleep. I am the usher and it was not his turn, I say this with certainty, knowing how random and cruel it all can be, he enjoyed music and fishing and camping and friends and I don't have to tell you that many people do not, by the end they do not, I will not, by my end, I will look forward only to seeing him if he recognizes me and I him. That we might not—oh, terrible thought. That death might change us irrevocably, make us new to each other like our dog after suffering a seizure sniffing our other dog as if meeting her for the first time. It was rather beautiful but I want nothing of newness with my son, I want to know him unceasingly.

⌇

He did not. He turned into the school parking lot.

⌇

I must surrender in my lifelong fight for beauty. I must claim I never wanted to win because winning doesn't teach you anything. What have you learned, then? I ask myself. Asking this is like grabbing my own shoulder to try to summon surprise. Looking in the mirror to try to see someone new. Touching my face like a stranger would, and the bounty of strangeness could be brought to me and a feast could be had.

⌇

I'm startled from a restless sleep by my neighbor's voice calling "Help!" and the engine of a car. I lie still. It can't be, I think. It can't be. I don't open the blinds or peer out the window. I don't do anything. The next day, I'm greatly relieved to see her getting into her car, but when she texts later to ask if I'd like to take a walk, I demur. I can't go on a walk with her because I can't tell her what I heard, hallucinatory scrap of her voice. I distance myself from her. I think I'll be able to see her again after enough time has passed that it won't matter what I didn't do, that what I didn't do will be lost under other things I did and didn't do, too many to sift through and single out the one done or undone deed that might've made the others possible. I see her coming and going, lemon-lime sandals one day, boots the next, the thump of the door, the purr of the engine. She seems perfectly fine. I'm the one who's hearing things. All night I lie listening to the house creaking, the doors rattling, the air parting, the airplanes rumbling in the empty stomach of the sky, all the laments that go unrecorded.

❧

In the daytime, the small planes putter antiquely. The shapeless takes on shape. The ominous dissipates. The gestures are contradictory.

❧

A friend and I talk on the phone for two hours. We live on opposite sides of the country. She says she's never been interested in writing women characters because she's not interested in writing about the body, and I think that's true, to write women is to write the body, and am briefly ashamed of my characters and their fettered flesh. Imagine a mind like an unplanted bulb, not yet shoved into soil and patted down, not yet sprinkled with fertilizer and flooded with water and light, the genius of how indisputably it exists without. To be a woman is to suffer the most intimate associations with the self. I make soft groaning noises when I get dressed in the morning, or when I change into my swimsuit. I hear these noises as if they're coming from someone else. I never quite *want* to go swimming until I'm pushing off the wall, unzippering the water, weightless as a boy.

～

My son rises late and pads around on bare feet with long, wild nails. I trap him and take him to the video store downtown, a beloved, cavernous institution going rapidly extinct. Near the entrance there's a popcorn machine that we help ourselves from, scooping stale popcorn into crimped paper bags. Thus equipped, we separate and wander the aisles of videos and DVDs. Smell of salt and mildew. Slumped shoulders dreaming over covers, scanning shelves. We might be lost in time here. We might never emerge. Maybe there's a storage room where our futures unspool on filmstrip, flicker to life under the coaxing of a projectionist with oily fingertips. The whirr, the cone of condensed light. I pass a couple in conference, their voices rising. Humphrey Bogart's on the ceiling-mounted TV grabbing an actress's upper arms, shaking her, slapping her across the face, pulling her to him, and squashing his clenched mouth onto hers. The only pure love is between mother and son.

～

A Russian sunbathes in the park across from our house. He lies on his stomach as if whispering to something inside the earth. I imagine him reading Tatyana Tolstaya's *Aetherial Worlds* to it. "This isn't the right place for me. Once again it's not right. I should know by now that the right place is inaccessible; maybe it exists in the past, over the green hills, or maybe it's drowned, or, perhaps, it hasn't materialized yet." And the residents of the underworld are consoled.

~

Walking past a white brick house with a glorious tangle of scarlet bougainvillea heaped over the garage, I see the old woman who lives there making her way to the sidewalk to retrieve her newspaper with a claw-shaped trash picker. In another person's hands I might think this implement terrible. The old woman's yard is dotted with crisp succulents and butterfly bushes. A lamp glows from her front window. I'm on the other side of the street and I slow, watching to be sure. She plucks the paper from the sidewalk, tucks it under her arm, waves, and goes back inside where I imagine she boils water for tea, sits down in lamplight, unfolds the paper.

~

I can't let her feel pain or fear. Even minor complaint would puncture my illusion.

~

Is it my mind or my eyes playing tricks on me when I read in a poem by Franz Wright the word *winter* instead of *summer* and *face* instead of *fate* and have to go back to the beginning and start again? I'm distracted by the status of the knobs on the stove and the locks on the door. The fate of the dog pricks me—does he have the blanket he likes to sleep on?—and the fate of the world, too. I manage to make it through a few stanzas and I'm feeling good, feeling like old times when reading took me in its giant's hand and held me aloft and showed me all of human endeavoring, all we could do and all we could lose, and I watched with pure animal contentment. Now it's different. Words slip and skitter away, my limbs stiffen. I begin to sweat. When I get into this state I must be very quiet. I must put my book aside and close the bedroom door silently, silently I must turn off the lamp with its difficult switch. I must be a ghost who puts herself to sleep by saying that everything has already happened, there is nothing left to do. I must summon the specter of the end in order to loosen my grip on the happening. It's not an easy trick, for I know there is always something left to do.

～

Hours online staring at pictures of people throughout history. My search is too broad, clearly.

～

Sometimes I think I'll leave town, become the caretaker of a property that I'll rent out, thus financing my escape. Of course, a shelter for me will be necessary, a barn or garage, somewhere to crouch, sleep, eat sandwiches, apples, listen with the teeth of my skin to branches scraping the roof. An outlet to plug in a space heater, and blinds to cover the windows unless they're very dusty.

～

A writer that my husband and I know has published a story collection containing stories that appeared in literary journals in the early '90s, and I love this man for holding on to his stories for so long, holding them shyly inside him. I think about this as I fall asleep, the patience of it, the extraordinary loyalty, the way the stories lay in wait all those years, quietly, quiet as shadows, unread X-rays, the silent curvature of whale bones at the bottom of the sea, and when I wake I pick up this thought right where I left off only now it's outside of me, less urgent and more discernible, an act instead of poetry.

⤚

A woman leaving the pool as I get there tells me to backstroke because the clouds are beautiful this morning, and they are, coolly floating in a tepid blue.

⤚

I love doubt. I'm not sure how I feel about certainty.

⤚

Certainty is like a closed door. Doubt leaves a way open.

⤚

A lodge in the snowy foothills of Ohio's Appalachian mountains. A weekend there before I was married, with my husband-to-be, my mother, my uncle, my cousin and his girlfriend. A weekend of hikes, board games, fires, single beds. It began to snow lightly as we left. We started down the mountain, my uncle driving, and almost immediately went into a skid. It happened very quickly, an untethered skate forward as if the laws of physics, the forces that grate against other forces, had disappeared, as if we traveled on the bands of a frozen waterfall, and then the nose of the car hit a skinny tree. The world resumed itself. We got out. My husband-to-be pulled my mother up the steep incline, new snow over old snow, to the road, and I clambered after them and saw how nearly we had come to sliding right off the mountain. We walked back to the lodge and I bought a tampon from a dispenser. Later we learned that the car's tires were completely bald. Only the tree had saved us.

❧

A few years later I left a hose on at the beginning of winter. The water froze and created an ice rink in the backyard. In the spring, I received a bill from the water company for nine hundred dollars. It was more than we could afford but I didn't think to contest it. For I had, hadn't I? Done what they said?

❧

I read that most avalanche victims are buried by less than three feet of snow, which must be heavier than it sounds. Imagine the booming of the snow, its white cape flung out and down, its frozen folds, the terrible plumage of its powder. Imagine the darkness, the clicking and final shifting of crystals. Imagine the silence of waiting to be found. Death is the search party that searches for you all your life. You hear it off in the distance, calling gently at first and then with less sympathy, less patience, with an urgency that seems gratuitous. Death is a figure in Gore-Tex, high-stepping it through the backcountry, brutal in how sensibly it's dressed. It will come even for those of us who live in sunny climates, in suburbs, among flowering trees.

❧

My father bikes past the jacarandas in square loops of four or five blocks, around and around. I wave to him, but he doesn't see me. He stares straight ahead and bikes slowly down the center of the street, wearing a white helmet and wide-legged trousers. If I wave vociferously enough he'll wave back, but I don't think he recognizes me. He's gotten hit by cars twice and twice walked away with scratches. The second time, he tells me what happened in a laughing, theatrical voice. She had her son in the back seat, he says of the driver, as if to prove that she wasn't paying attention. She called an ambulance even though he said he didn't need one, and they bandaged him curbside. My son was in a car that was hit by another car recently. They had just pulled away from a four-way stop. He screamed at the girl who was driving to brake, and she did, but not before the other car smashed into their front right side, shearing off the bumper, scattering the license plate. It was like that cliché about time slowing down, he said. It really does. It really did. We were listening to old Alex G. The songs before everyone knew him.

A Lot of Good It Does Being
in the Underworld

Says an unsavory character in *The Stranger*, which I'm rereading to see how it strikes me now. By underworld, he means a group of petty criminals, but I think the sentiment applies to the place, too. It's not damnation that sends you there. It's the instinct for return.

When I heard that my friend was dead, I thought back to our exchange of texts the week before. We had planned to meet at a fish restaurant for lunch and her death seemed impossible with this plan unrealized. I believed in plans, in the adhesive property of the calendar, and while I could fathom a last-minute rescheduling—I rescheduled many plans myself—I could not fathom utter obviation, a voiding of the future as if it were a thing that could simply be stamped out. My friend lived on a mountain and I lived in a valley. The restaurant was located roughly halfway between our houses. We had met there before. It had a scuffed black-and-white tile floor and milk glass ceiling lamps and the waiters wore broadcloth shirts and long black aprons. Despite its gesturing toward authenticity it could not shake its mantle of corporate arrangement, and we took solace in its anonymity. There, my friend ordered iced tea and broiled grouper while I ordered a messy, dripping kaiser roll sandwich. Lemon seeds in little puddles of water at the bases of our glasses.

That was five years ago at least. I'd told myself I'd contact her again when I had news to announce, an awful way of thinking about friendship, as if it existed only out in the open rather than in the underground life of shared sympathies. Eventually I did have some modest news, and I sent out a group email and she replied and that's how we fell back in touch.

After we arranged our lunch date we kept texting. We had both read Louise Glück's new collection of poems, her twelfth or thirteenth, and we discussed a particular poem, a particular line of that poem, *You must ask yourself if you deceive yourself,* which I'd read as *You must ask yourself if you **deserve** yourself,* and my friend had read as *You must ask yourself if you **desert** yourself.* How funny, how strange! we agreed, and then I said I thought my misreading got to the nature of womanhood itself, and my friend said her misreading was about the human desire for oblivion. To be a woman is more specific than to be a human, I responded. My friend did not reply, and that was the last I heard from her.

She was magnetic in the way of a being whose balance on earth is unsteady but the way she flaps across the axis, her arms out at her sides and bracelets rattling, utterly transfixing.

What feeling would you least want to elicit in others? I once asked her. Pity, my friend replied.

She never did. Admiration, concern, puzzlement, gratitude. Her students loved her very much.

We taught at the same university and then we didn't any longer—that's the simplest explanation for why we stopped seeing each other—but I admit it had become confusing to be with her. She was always complimenting me, flattering me, making too much of small things. It was embarrassing and had, in fact, the opposite effect of what she intended, for I began to suspect myself of such demonstrable fragility that she thought I needed shoring up. I wonder now if she wasn't simply trying to deflect attention from herself, from the substance of her days. Eventually she would relay some event or drama but the hyperbole continued, warping the proportions of what she said, pulling like an undertow against the stability of her story, a discernible chronology, a series of recognizable acts. I knew my friend thought what she was saying was true, and knew too that in some crucial way it was not. So when she told me about the time she abandoned her car at the side of a mountain road, and no one knew where she was, and the pills she had in her possession, I did not seize upon it. Instead, I exclaimed almost in *awe* at her confession, as if a monstrous feathered thing had brushed past me. That is to say, I understood her confession, but I pushed that understanding deep inside of me, just as I buried so many other unpleasant revelations.

Now, a month after her death, I stand in front of the building where my office is, among the careful colorful shrubbery. Two young women walk past me wearing high-waisted jeans and indomitable expressions, a kick-assery somewhat undercut by their ardent clutching of their phones, and I think of my friend and how much pain we had ahead of us at that age, and how we didn't know it, and wonder what we'd have done differently had we known. Every young woman is captive to a painful future that she must not, cannot, see clearly, for if she did she would only try futilely to avoid it. It is futile even if her future is also filled with joy, as ours were. For the future doesn't end with joy—there is always a moment after, even if the joy is stronger than what comes next.

I stop reading for the classes I'm teaching and read poetry instead. Novels seem bloated and unnecessary, their tissue and ligaments, characters saying things. Whereas a poem is the declaration itself.

It's simple. It speaks. There is no need for continuity.

My friend slips from my mind for a day or two at a time and

then returns from another angle, and I see her standing next to the elevator in the building where we taught, a different building on a different, duller campus, smiling, blinking behind her glasses, all blurry blue eyeliner and tall leather boots. The boots were catastrophically expensive, my friend told me. She stashed a flask in one of them. This was discovered later.

During this time, my friend emailed a manuscript to me, a memoir she'd written about the year she spent in Nova Scotia when she was twenty-two. I had difficulty understanding her poetry, which was highly referential and elaborate, each line so baroque something essential was obscured. Her memoir, however, was different. It was lucid, revelatory, filled with longing like a stream, a living, running thing. I encouraged her to publish it, but she never did. I suspected she was protecting her husband, for men are sensitive about old loves, or maybe she had other reasons, or maybe she did try to publish it and wasn't able to, but I don't think so.

Some words carry so much awareness inside them I can't read them at night, I can only read them during the day. For their awareness makes me aware. That's how I felt reading my friend's manuscript. That she was finally telling the truth, and the truth requires a response.

I decide to try to get the manuscript published posthumously. I look for it but I can't find it, and I realize it may be on an old laptop, a laptop that won't turn on but that I haven't recycled because of my fear it may still hold something important, an importance all the more significant because I can't get to the important thing, so I email her friend in another state to ask if she has a copy of it. My friend's friend takes a long time to reply, and when she does she says she doesn't have a copy of it, and that our friend never showed it to her or even mentioned it. It's as if she thinks I'm inventing the manuscript's existence, and I wonder if she's aggrieved that our friend shared something with me that she did not share with her. That might've contributed to the slowness of her response, though she would if asked say that she was grieving, overwhelmed, overworked.

I email the editor of the press that published my friend's first book to see if she might have the manuscript. She does not. She says I should absolutely submit it if I find it, and they open for submissions for three and a half hours on January 4.

I don't know what people do all day long. This is the well of mystery I draw from.

I think about it a lot. The rhythms, rationales, ways of being of other people. My husband tells me not to try to understand, but I do. I can't help myself. The incredible mystery and loneliness of being someone else.

I wish I could've seen my friend age. Seen her as an old lady.

When I heard about her death I also heard that she was not married anymore.

Years ago, we got very drunk with our husbands and another couple. My husband and I had arranged for our son to stay with my parents for the night, and my friend's sons were staying with her parents, and the other couple did not yet have children, though they too would have a son. I was wearing a dress—I rarely do—and I saw my friend's husband notice me for the first time, saw that I had risen to float above the vision he usually had of me to present something that he liked, a certain carefree manner that stood naked with possibility. We had a drink, and went out to dinner and had a few more, and returned to our house and continued drinking. At some point we jumped into the pool wearing our clothes. I yanked my arms out of my dress. The pool was turbulent with bodies, and I was pushed into the deep end where I lost my bearings and went under. Someone cupped my breast. When I came back up, my dress slung around my neck, my friend was on the deck, weaving toward the house with a private decisiveness.

My husband and the others were toweling off. Inside, I found my friend passed out on the kitchen floor.

The other couple shared a glass of water and drove off.

We tried to stop them, didn't we?

The last time I saw my friend was on the Fourth of July. I dislike the Fourth of July. It's a hot holiday, a brazen holiday, but when you have children you feel you must do things, so we took them to a celebration at a park while our husbands remained at home, drinking beer and grilling salmon.

Old people stood around under a tent making pancakes. This wasn't what I wanted to be doing with her. She stood out among all the wandering, fervid, sun-scorched people. Tall and graceful, necklaces slippery with sweat.

Our children slid down a large inflated water slide with a couple of hoses running rivulets down the middle. Some friends came over and I introduced her. I was proud to be in the company of someone so beautiful.

The slide required tickets but no one was collecting them so we let the children go again and again, their skin screeching against the plastic, swim trunks sagging, feet muddy from the two scoops of puddles that had formed at the bottom of the slide. Their pleasure was so exorbitant it became ours in a way. Finally we left and walked home past the large houses, down the wide street where the parade would soon travel, where low lawn chairs lined the grassy sidewalk strip and you had only embrace what we could not— cheap hope—to the street of smaller houses where my husband and I lived.

False Choice

If only she had packing tape. If only she had a cut-up cantaloupe and a waffle weave shower curtain.

If only people wouldn't park their cars in the lot near her house and eat their fast food and open their doors and plunk their containers right there on the ground for the coyotes.

If only she had cork-soled sandals and palazzo pants.

Maybe she's still assembling herself, while those who seem to have it all are in fact passive, stagnant, spoiling.

Maybe she'll write a podcast . . .

There is always this tension: to crisply replicate reality or to listen to the burr and hum of sentences and follow them to their sometimes illogical conclusions. But it's a false choice. To force logic into the shape of abandon, that's what she'd like to do.

In her little notebook, a line from *Sleepless Nights*: "She was forever like one watched over by wakefulness in her deepest sleep."

To be aware, always, that she's sleeping . . . to be aware, always, that she's aware . . . that there's something *beyond* her, a skin outside her body, a shadow built by the walls of herself.

She remembers a girl from long ago who she'd see in the computer lab now and then—when she sat at a keyboard it was as if at meditation. To glimpse her in this one placid action, she became a symbol, reassuring, until one day she never saw the girl again, and then she became a symbol of something else.

Time's passing. How small the faces of her youth grow.

Often she assumes a happiness or contentment in other people that they do not, in fact, possess. Two of the couples she's compared her marriage to unfavorably have gotten divorced in the last year. Her husband likes to remind her of this.

If only her husband would hold her hand when they went on walks, or touch the small of her back when they entered restaurants. How lovely, a relationship predicated on one person treating the other like an invalid. Of course, invalids have to lie around all day and not do much.

But the *minds* of invalids—roiled, fevered things swimming with visions while hers is made of to-do lists.

Brown mountains in the near distance. The sun a fist opening and closing, pumping light through the air.

In her little notebook, a line from Kate Chopin: "She did not stop to ask if it were or were not a monstrous joy that held her."

One eye feasts, the other famines.

If only she'd ordered more pairs of nude-colored underwear. Two more, to be precise.

She remembers the sounds of her childhood: *The Music Man*, Joan Baez, applause from *The Oprah Winfrey Show*. When what she wanted was for someone to sit and tell her secrets.

Highway noises slide through the night like beads on a wire. When it's cold outside, when the air is clear the engines of the unfortunates come right into her room and she rides with them in thrall to the tinfield spray of dashboard lights, the stench and smoke of the upholstery.

Being influenced, the poet W. S. Merwin says, isn't a matter of reading something on the page and trying to replicate it. It's a matter of listening with your body, taking the words inside you. The rhythm of sentences, their rushes and pauses, starts and stops, the chewy beauty of language—this is what I hope to bring to life with these readings (from an old syllabus).

The plan was to read a poem or a passage from a story to her students at the beginning of each class. She never did. She doesn't remember now why she discarded the idea. She thinks of all the passages she didn't read and how Joan Didion said what's so hard about the first sentence is that you're stuck with it and Christos Ikonomou said he has to believe what he writes is true not real reality is different from truth and Olga Tokarczuk said the narrated sin will be forgiven and the narrated life saved. She'd meant to say these things, too.

This Isn't the Actual Sea

As I approached my friend's house, I could see by the number of cars on the street that many people had been invited, far more than I expected. I considered turning around. Instead, I let myself in to a clamor of voices and the barking of her poodle. The long living room windows swam with gusts of color as guests circled in their bright sweaters. "Come here," my friend said. "You look older! And I thought you were timeless." She hugged me and I hugged her back. When I pulled away my ring snagged in her hair.

I apologized. "It was silly that we went so long without seeing each other," she said, dipping her head as I disentangled the ring, like a child letting its mother work out a knot. When she raised her head she smiled over my shoulder at someone. "You embarrassed me."

I pulled two long, crinkled strands of her hair from the ring, a flat, square, algae-green-and-black-speckled stone, set in gold. It wasn't my wedding ring. My husband and I didn't wear wedding rings. Mine gave me a rash, his he'd misplaced sink-side in a restaurant in LA, gone by the time we went back. The thought of wearing someone else's wedding ring seemed unlucky to me, darkly incantatory. (Probably it had been sold.) We'd decided not to replace it, and now, as I released my friend's hair from between my pinched fingers and watched it drift to the ground, I wondered if this made us weak or strong, reckless in our indifference to the totems of our pairing. My friend moved to the center of the room and thanked everyone for coming, and I took a seat on the couch sandwiched between two others. The poodle was sprawled on the floor in the middle of everyone, and people would reach out their arms and legs occasionally and give him a swipe. Guests leaned against walls, crowded out of the kitchen. It was a happy, eager group, willing to give themselves over to art, to be transformed by an encounter with what they would remember later as intellectual beauty. One always remembers one's first time with intellectual beauty.

"It's been twenty years since I did this," my friend said. "I was twenty-nine when my first film was released. I never expected it to be received the way it was, I never thought it would become something of a cult favorite. It took on a life of its own as I married, raised twins, saw them off to college. Recently, at a party, I overheard someone talking about it. He thought it was Peter Bogdanovich."

A redheaded man raised a tremulous hand. "That was me. Sorry. I thought it was his juvenilia."

"I told myself what I'd had was enough," my friend continued. "Why would I deserve anything more? No one expected a second film from me, and for a long time it seemed as if there wouldn't be one. I'm not going to say I was writing even when I wasn't, because I don't know what that means. The truth is more like I *wasn't* writing even when I was. I'd start something and it would turn into a to-do list . . ." Her voice trailed off and she gestured toward a white bedsheet unfurled in front of the fireplace. "And then this came to me. I give you *The Park.*"

The lights dimmed, and the movie began playing. It doesn't matter, just now, what it was about. When it was over, everyone applauded and thronged my friend to congratulate her. They told her how much they cared about the characters, how they didn't expect to care so much but she had forced them to. The darkness outside was now complete and I was reminded of a sensation from early childhood, of waking from a nap and feeling that the heart, the dense bud of the day had disappeared and I was left with misplaced time, an hour I didn't recognize, silty and mournful and gray.

My friend took my elbow and drew me into the kitchen. "Did you like it?" she said. "I thought it would be different this time, but it's not. If anything it's worse because I'm older. I should know better."

I told her I did. I said these quartz countertops were the pathetic kingdom of doubt, and she must leave it, she must leave it forever. "If behind every great man is a woman, behind every woman is a panting blob of insecurity, a——"

"It's not that." My friend shook her head. "I just think it sort of sucked."

"It did not suck," a man who'd approached silently said. Our heads rolled in his direction.

"I don't mean *sucked* sucked," my friend said.

"Oh, false modesty, I've missed you! You're a relic like a shard of pottery or something." To make sure she got the friendly spirit of his delivery, he reached out and cupped her arm.

She laughed. "Here lies the museum of false modesty. Do you have a ticket?"

I slunk away.

I couldn't fall asleep that night. "Let's have sex," I said to my husband, but he didn't like the way I broached the subject, and we quarreled. I rose from bed and scuffed into Birkenstocks and walked outside to the park across the street from our house. Leaves massed above me like filigreed clouds. Trash cans waited to be emptied, filled. Their inhuman patience leveled my racing heart. I, too, had given things to the world—let's say poems, but they could be stories or novels or simply my opinions—that I felt, immediately, I wanted to take back, and hated with a sickening intimacy. Why did I feel that way? Here is the shuddering dark inside of my brain, these things seemed to say. Here is my religion. Bear in mind I am not religious.

My friend and I had avoided seeing each other in order to avoid false-hood, because to not speak of what had caused our break would be a lie. To not speak of what we had gleaned of one another, for while I had seen vulnerability in her so had I seen an adherence to hierar-chy, to an idea of who should do her bidding and how that bidding should be done, while, for her part, she had seen something stub-born, disloyal, in me. To speak of this would expose us to scrutiny and take every last bit of her strength, the strength she was using to make her movie. It was only after she'd finished, when she had proof of some sort, that she decided she could see me again. The proof wasn't the movie, it was the survival of her secret self. After all, her friends weren't making movies, the woman who taught her yoga class wasn't making a movie, the twins weren't making movies, her ex-husband wasn't making a movie, the neighbors who stopped her for small talk weren't making movies, and so she, the she they knew, the she in the material world, wasn't making a movie, either. It was some hidden, grotesque part of her, some immaterial urge that roiled inside her like steam in a bottle that was making a movie. She must've known that there were other women out there who were making movies (and seen some of those movies, the few that eked through), she just didn't know the women personally. She texted me the next day, a Saturday.

That guy
False modesty guy?

Got xx what a rando
Listen to you with the youth's lingo.
Yes cheap perfect words
I shut my phone in a drawer and ate a yogurt and tried to work.
When I checked it again after what felt like half an hour, nine minutes had passed. I was rewarded with an invitation for coffee.

How different a house looked after a party, its facade flattened, washed of responsibility. In the kitchen, the poodle sniffed my crotch until I pushed his head away. The coffeemaker burbled, my friend poured. She placed two steaming mugs on the breakfast table, a sugar bowl, cream. Her hair was pulled back with a tortoiseshell clip. Her ears were very pink, and I was reminded of the peppermint pig my husband brought forth each Christmas after dinner. He placed the pig in a velvet bag, and invited our son to smash it with a little silver hammer. It was a tradition from his childhood—eating a piece of the pig was supposed to mean you'd be prosperous in the year ahead, but I rebelled against the idea of treating prosperity like something to be heralded, hoped for, coaxed forth with rituals. Give me insight, I always thought as I let the peppermint dissolve in my mouth, which was in its own way as rapacious, an invisible acquisition, sometimes undependable.

"You left early last night," my friend said.

"I made way."

"I know, I'd never met him before, a friend brought him. Afterward I cried from some kind of ancient exhaustion and we ate leftovers."

"Which leftovers?"

"Those almond horns."

"And then you felt better?"

"About me. I won't see him again. I'm over it, the drama. Give me a good meal, good weather, a comfortable bed."

"You already have those things."

"The weather's only mine when it's bad," she said.

"I know what you mean."

"We're so *blind*," my friend said exultantly.

I felt very close to her then.

My friend couldn't stand the idea of her movie being ignored or reviewed. Both scenarios were terrible to her. Being ignored would confirm her invisibility, while being reviewed would dissect her presence. Her movie played at a few art house theaters in New York (but not at any of the Laemmles here), and when she found out it was to be reviewed in the Sunday *New York Times*, she asked me to come over and read the review first. I did so with a mean need for it to be panned. If her movie was panned I would find some fuel for myself, a jagged pleasure. It wasn't panned. It was well reviewed, and I felt, too, genuine happiness for my friend, and shame at my animal thought.

I was sitting on her front stoop. She took the newspaper from me and read it herself and then rattled it decisively closed.

"It's too generous," she said.

"It's not. It's perceptive."

"You don't mean it. I can see it in your eyes."

"My eyes lie!"

"I think what I'm most afraid of is never having another original thought again."

Her street was lined with ginkgo trees that had turned yellow and were shedding their fan-shaped leaves. It was early December and fall had arrived. Even so, the cooler weather could erupt at any time into heat like the brush fires that broke out near highway exit ramps, long tongues of smoke in the distance. Now, though, the air was clear. Leaves plastered the sidewalk. I had once been afraid of the same thing, but I went so long without an original thought

I forgot what it was like; in my maze of the familiar I forgot how grand the strange could be.

I saw her in the grocery store. We were at opposite ends of the freezer where bags of fish were kept. I saw her ask an aproned clerk a question. I saw her not like how slow he was to respond for she brandished her phone in his face, causing him to step backward into someone else's cart. They both turned to this third person, an elderly woman who'd approached with fragile steps, and apologized profusely. I saw her face move from anger to concern, I saw how swiftly and shamelessly she camouflaged herself inside separate moments and the forces that made them. I saw her see me and come forward explaining before she even quite reached me that she'd had to scold the boy for scrolling at work. I asked if he might not have been searching for music, as my son so often claimed he was doing when I caught him gazing dumbly at his phone, and she said no, he was watching someone skateboard off a roof. "A roof!" my friend said, as if had it been stairs it might've been different. As if all human effort must go through her, her body a sieve with the heavy organs caught in the bowl of her and the rest running out.

She was invited to screen her movie at the women's college in our town, and she asked me to accompany her. The campus was a lush collection of bougainvillea- and fountain-filled courtyards that seemed designed less for the delights of the mind than of the senses, the plashing of water, the wax-paper weight of the sun. In a velvet auditorium, a professor of gender and sexuality studies introduced my friend. The lights dimmed and the movie began. Ten or fifteen minutes in, I became aware that students were leaving, swiftly up the aisles, the shushing of their leggings. Afterward, the professor opened the floor to questions. The questions asked by those students who remained were deeply skeptical of the movie's depiction of the lives of middle-aged women as lives of frustration and anger and shame. You could tell they didn't think their futures would bear any resemblance to that. Their futures were like stacks of soft-folded sweaters in a pretty store with a salesgirl whose hair was cut in a style they would soon see everywhere. Some girls were nearly soothsayers that way. The movie, no, the movie didn't feel that apt. It felt a little irrelevant to be honest.

My friend nodded vigorously as they spoke. She said she understood. She used to feel that way herself. But everything changes when you get married, she said. I thought of her ex, a slight man with slick lips who had disappeared early each morning onto a train that took him into LA to work at a podcast production company. The most shocking thing about him was that he was missing a nipple. My friend had felt he didn't take her seriously and had only tolerated her creative ambitions. I had a recurring fantasy about him, or not a fantasy exactly but a sequence of thoughts I summoned when I couldn't fall asleep: I was dying and asked to see him, and he walked into the dim room where I lay quietly, and held my hand and confessed his regret, and I realized I didn't have any regret and that was the great, the only gift of dying.

After the Q&A, we had dinner with the professor of sexuality and gender studies and her wife at an Italian restaurant. The professor apologized for the students. She said it was ironic, their objection to the vision of women the movie presented, for had my friend's movie depicted women as reduced figures in entirely functionary sexual roles they would've been down with that. My friend came to the students' defense. To the professor it must've seemed like generosity, but I knew the choice my friend was being asked to make was to align herself either with the bitterness of age or the glaze of youth, that sweet shellac that cracked in skittish lines at a fork tap. After dinner we walked home, politely drunk. She'd chosen the side with all the joys and disappointments still to come.

I understood what my friend's movie was about the first time I saw it, but I was too distracted by the other people in the room for it to sink in. It was only after my second viewing that I realized how little she'd changed about the incident that had caused us to stop seeing each other. It had happened shortly after her husband moved out, in those early weeks of her aloneness. She had asked me to dog-sit for a few days while she went to soothe herself at a hot springs. Of course I agreed. It was a midweek trip, so the poodle couldn't stay with her soon-to-be-ex. The poodle was used to having some-one around—it wouldn't work for him to be left alone all day. My friend dropped him and his bed and leash and kibble at my house on a Tuesday morning, and I told her to have a wonderful time. She was traveling to the hot springs with another of her friends, a woman I knew only slightly and who was so beautiful I felt like an old, cracked log in her presence.

Later that day, I decided to take the poodle to the dog park. It would be fun, I thought, to see him loping about and to pretend that he was mine. I loaded him into the car and we drove there, and there he bit a small dog, badly, on the neck. The small dog let out a cry like a peacock's, and gushed blood. My friend was very upset when I called her and told her what had happened. She drove straight home, came into my house, and dropped to her knees to inspect every inch of the poodle, who had sustained no injury and was lying in his bed panting with residual angst. My friend said she hadn't told me to take the poodle to the dog park, and I said I assumed it was some-where he had been before, and my friend said it was, and it had been fine, but she'd sensed the park's potential for chaos, for violence. But it was your dog's potential for violence you sensed, I said. My friend began to cry. She said I was selfish, a selfish person willing to blame others for their own suffering. Then she piled the poodle's leash and kibble into the dog bed, and left, the poodle trotting after her with hung head. He knew we were talking about him.

I had disavowed my relationship to the poodle right after he sank his teeth into the small dog's neck. The small dog's owner and I had been chatting so pleasantly before the attack. Oh my god! He's not mine! I had cried, though the small dog's owner was too busy kicking the poodle off her dog to respond.

Seeing my friend's movie a second time, I noted how brusquely the friend who was dog-sitting treated the dog after the attack, how completely she shunned the animal, and I realized that my friend identified with her dog very closely. I thought back to the attack again, trying to picture exactly what had happened, and I remembered that the small dog had sniffed the poodle under his muzzle right before the poodle bit him. Raised his little head and sniffed the soft, vulnerable throat so pink beneath the poodle's lambswool coat. The attack appeared unprovoked, but it wasn't. It wasn't justified, but it was not unprovoked.

As I swam laps, I considered how to talk to my friend about her movie. I knew she'd deny an explicit connection. If pressed, she might say a movie is a self-contained experience, and the filmmaker won't be around to explain it, so of course I was free to interpret it any way I liked. Putting it that way would undermine my authority quite nicely while seeming to argue for the autonomy of art and the independence of the viewer, for an authentic relationship between two entities that were both, in their own ways, staged. My friend might quote Gertrude Stein, who said she wrote for herself and strangers. I began to backstroke, droplets from my fingertips falling into my mouth. The ceiling panels were open to pale parcels of sky.

I emailed my friend's ex-husband to ask if he'd seen her movie. He had not been at her house, and I didn't know if that was because he hadn't been invited, or had declined to come. (My husband had declined to come.) I wrote *I felt it didn't imagine enough*, filled with a sudden desire to commiserate with someone who must, himself, wish my friend had done more work creating rather than replicating, building something new. I sent the email before I could stop myself. He replied politely, with no sympathy.

My friend was raking leaves in her driveway, her car parked in the street and the poodle sniffing about the yard. It had rained the night before, and the mountains were covered with snow. Palm trees in the foreground, white mountains in the background, the sky a heart-rending blue. I sat on her stoop and said the name of her ex.

"What about him?" she said.

"Do you see him regularly?"

"We're very friendly." She turned her head and called to the poodle, then turned back to me. "We don't have to explain ourselves anymore. We can be more generous."

I had heard this before, or some version of it, and indeed it made sense that those who had suffered divorce's pain would also want to broadcast its freedoms. Like swimming in an icy lake and feeling very alive, very awake, in intimate contact with the elements. A genuine feeling, an admirable one, though I wouldn't for any reason, not for clarity or moral forthrightness or inner rectitude, choose an icy lake over my eighty-two-degree pool. She called the poodle again more sharply, and he came and sat at her feet and despite this act of obedience, or because of it, she picked up his leash from where it lay coiled next to me and leashed him.

"Why do you ask?" she said.

"I've been thinking about him for some reason. And you. You seemed so happy together."

She snorted. "You can't know what it's like to be another person, not really. This is what we depend on."

She loved Ingmar Bergman, especially *Wild Strawberries*. I objected to his depiction of women. She said that to dramatize an ideal, one always exaggerated. I said ideals were for cowards. She said my thinking was too grim. I said hers was too accommodating, stretching to fit the flatness she had been given and asked to believe was profundity. She said I needed to smile more. I said that was what men always said about women. She said that was because unsmiling women scared men, but she wasn't a man and I didn't scare her. Why then? I said. You just look better when you do, she said. Bergman and Fellini and Cassavetes and Coppola and Anderson and Fincher, all that male weather, sun storm, deluge, drought, downpour.

And then came a few weeks during which we did not see each other, for no reason. Just a stretch of being idle. But I was aware as the weeks went by that although there had been no incident this time, every day we did not see each other brought us closer to never see-ing each other again. How telling myself I'd be fine before—when we really weren't seeing each other—meant in fact I would be fine, though something would be lost. How you can lose something and still be fine. How the lost thing is more present when it's lost.

Sometimes my thinking about her was clear, thrillingly absolute. Sometimes my thinking was laden with regret. One might say it was really about myself though it felt so precisely about her.

I was driving into the foothills, listening to an interview with Bruce Springsteen on the radio. He was saying when he first met his wife they had so much in common. "It was like, before you were you, you were me," he said. I stopped at a red light. A car with a loud muffler pulled up next to mine and rumbled in place and when the light changed took off in a series of ignominious putts. The road rose and narrowed. We go to music not to learn something but to be reminded of something, Springsteen said, and I turned onto the street where I'd arranged to meet my friend, parked, and got out. She was leaning against her car, staring at the mountains. She had brought water and I hadn't, and I imagined asking her for water, whether I could or whether it would seem too forward, drinking out of the same spout. We donned hats and set out and I determined to trudge through my thirst. She began to talk about her movie, about how she was trying to scare up more interest in it. Attention wasn't something she wanted, but needed. She supposed it was the people who wanted it that got it. She was grateful her movie had been reviewed in the *Times*, but it hadn't been reviewed anywhere else. No one had approached her for an interview, no film festivals had contacted her, and her window of relevance was shrinking every day.

"My little performance at Shelton College might be it," she said.

I mentioned that I knew an editor who might be interested. In reality, I knew no such person. "Send me a link," I said.

"Thanks. I'll give you a DVD, too." We were climbing on loose, pebbly dirt past gray-blue agaves and manzanita trees whose dried-blood bark seemed to run in rivulets down the trunks.

"You know, I've been thinking a lot about what I said to you in the kitchen that night. I was wrong," she said. "I'm better than many. I'm downright good. If they can be, why not me?"

I told her I agreed. I said her next movie would be her best, meaning it as a compliment, meaning it would be more elusive, more mysterious, that it would range farther afield and might surprise her, but it sounded as if I were saying that what she'd made wasn't enough. To make up for it I decided to tell her about what I was working on now. She had given me this story and I realized she could take it back by uttering two or three condemnatory words, or smiling with a little question mark at the corners of her mouth, or allowing a veil of disinterest to come into her eyes. We walked higher and higher until we had a view of the valley, cars swimming through the milky smog, flitting close behind one another like fish in an aquarium about whom one inevitably thinks, Do they know this isn't the actual sea? Then we walked back to our cars and I followed her to her house and idled out front while she ran inside. She reemerged and handed a DVD to me through the car window, and I could hear the poodle barking and smell something coming off her, a stab of deodorant, a sort of unnatural hope and exertion, and I felt then the terror and promise of friendship, the daily encounter with what the other dares to be.

Acknowledgments

I'm grateful to the editors of the journals in which these stories first appeared: "Traveling Light" in *Prairie Schooner*; "Something in Common" in *Story*; "Falconer" in the *Virginia Quarterly Review*; "A Neighboring State" in the *Normal School*; "The Artist's Wife" in the *Georgia Review*; "Origin Story" in *McSweeney's*; "Dogwood" in *LitMag*; "A Lot of Good It Does Being in the Underworld" in *A Public Space*; "False Choice" in *StoryQuarterly*; and "This Isn't the Actual Sea" in the *Idaho Review* and *The Best American Short Stories 2023*.

I'm enormously grateful to Carmen Giménez and Matthew Vollmer.

Thank you to Ethan Nosowsky, Katie Dublinski, Brittany Torres Rivera, and everyone at Graywolf Press. Thank you to Min Jin Lee, Heidi Pitlor, Claudia Ballard, Ellen Reyes, and Oscar's shirt.

Fond thanks to Jessica Anthony, Brock Clarke, Karen Anderson, Jerry Gabriel, Stacy Elliott, Kirsten Suttner, Rebecca Kornbluh, Katherine Friedman, Marcella Zita, Amy Barrett, Abby Brown, and Kelly Pender. And to Julie Paegle.

Thank you to my family of writers: my father, brother, uncle, and first cousin once removed, the California Priest. And to my family of readers: my mother and grandmother.

Above all I'm grateful to my husband, Kevin Moffett, and our son, Ellis, for their stellar sense of humor and for their love.

Corinna Vallianatos is the author of *My Escapee*, winner of the Grace Paley Prize for Short Fiction, and the novel *The Beforeland*. Her work has appeared in *The Best American Short Stories 2023*, *McSweeney's*, *A Public Space*, and elsewhere. A MacDowell Fellow, Vallianatos lives in Virginia.

Graywolf Press publishes risk-taking, visionary writers who transform culture through literature. As a nonprofit organization, Graywolf relies on the generous support of its donors to bring books like this one into the world.

This publication is made possible, in part, by the voters of Minnesota through a Minnesota State Arts Board Operating Support grant, thanks to a legislative appropriation from the arts and cultural heritage fund. Significant support has also been provided by other generous contributions from foundations, corporations, and individuals. To these supporters we offer our heartfelt thanks.

MINNESOTA
STATE ARTS BOARD

CLEAN
WATER
LAND &
LEGACY
AMENDMENT

To learn more about Graywolf's books and authors
or make a tax-deductible donation, please visit
www.graywolfpress.org.

The text of *Origin Stories* is set in Perpetua MT Pro.
Book design by Rachel Holscher.
Composition by Bookmobile Design & Digital Publisher
Services, Minneapolis, Minnesota.
Manufactured by Versa Press on acid-free,
30 percent postconsumer wastepaper.